Beguiling

Bridget

by

Leah Sanders &
Rachel Van Dyken

Beguiling Bridget
by Leah Sanders & Rachel Van Dyken
Published by Astraea Press
www.astraeapress.com

BEGUILING BRIDGET
Copyright © 2012 LEAH SANDERS & RACHEL VAN DYKEN
ISBN 13: 978-1493726646
ISBN: 1493726641
Cover Art Designed by Bryan Griffin
Edited by Stephanie Taylor

Prologue
History Repeats Itself

"Anthony?" The shock in Ambrose's voice was unmistakable, though in hindsight Anthony wasn't really sure if it was his twin brother speaking or a beautiful woman with facial hair.

He was that foxed.

"Can you hear me?" His brother's voice was something akin to a loud screeching, causing a resounding shriek to pump through his ears until he thought he might be fit for Bedlam.

"'Course you can't hear me," Ambrose scoffed then waved away the proprietor. "Never saw you drink so much in my entire life, and that includes the time when you tried to drink Wilde under the table at the annual debutante ball. Those women sure hadn't seen a man dance a waltz with such..." He paused as if trying to think of the correct way to say something insulting. "...Reckless abandon, that's for sure." His twin patted his back. "Now tell me, why is it that I find you here, of all places, drinking away your sorrows? Aren't you to be fighting Wilde in a duel?"

Anthony lifted his pounding head to glare into his brother's eyes. "I'll kill him."

"That's the spirit." Ambrose motioned for a drink and took a seat. "Now, what is this about? Did he steal your horse? Give you another dirty look? Oh no, wait. I have it." He snapped his fingers in the air. "Did he sneeze into your favorite whiskey again? I do know how you hate that. It's so inconvenient to have to pour good whiskey out, wouldn't you agree?" Ambrose winked and threw back the contents of his glass.

Anthony steadied himself in his seat and fought against the anger pouring through his body at alarming speeds. "He stole her."

"So we are talking about your horse, then?" Ambrose seemed relieved as he relaxed against the back of his chair.

"No, it's not about a blasted horse. He stole *her*! The woman I was supposed to marry. Stole her right from under me, like the sod he is."

"So you were, er... on her... and he... um..." Ambrose flushed.

Anthony swore. "No, you idiot. Not in that... capacity." He surprised himself by being able to think of large words, let alone use them, in his inebriated state. "I saw them. Together... kissing."

"Well, I do hope you alerted the Bow Street runners. We can't have rakes running about town deflowering women, if you get my meaning."

"This isn't a jest, Ambrose! It wasn't *some* woman!"

"Let me guess." His brother leaned in. "You're jealous because Wilde kissed a girl you had deep feelings for. Well, plenty of fish in the sea, my friend!" He hit him on the back, setting Anthony teetering off the chair.

Mustering as much strength as his aching body would allow, Anthony rose to his full height. Impressive that it was, he knew his body would pay for it later. "I love her!" he announced loudly.

Silence followed in the establishment.

Ambrose's eyes widened. "Just whom are we talking about?"

"Lady Bridget. I love her, and Wilde was kissing her... I'll kill him."

Just then the door blew open. Ambrose turned around with a grin on his face. "Here we go. I do love duels. Did you know..." he addressed the proprietor, "we were here just last year under similar circumstances? Only it was my brother and I fighting a duel, and, well, I didn't exactly go through with it..."

"Ah." The gentleman smiled. "I remember the story. Tell me, how is the missus?"

"Oh fine, fine." Ambrose shrugged and turned toward Wilde.

Wilde's eyes were trained on Anthony. A wild fervor of hate that Anthony had never seen before in his friend seemed to radiate from him.

"I'll kill you for ruining my only chance with her! And I will defend her honor!" Wilde yelled, pushing people out of the way as he blazed a path toward Anthony.

"Me?" Anthony puffed up his chest. "If your chances are ruined it is only because she has seen you for who you truly are! It is I who has been wronged! How dare you steal her from me!"

"Steal?" Wilde repeated, shocking Anthony. He had never seen his friend's composure rattled so much.

"I never stole a thing in my life! If you're looking for the thief and scoundrel, you have no further to look than the mirror, my friend!"

"Gentlemen, please." Ambrose stepped in, obviously offended, considering he saw the same reflection in his mirror.

"Why don't we settle this away from the crowds, eh?

Without pistols?"

"I'll fight for her," Wilde said plainly.

Anthony closed his eyes against the vision of Wilde kissing the only woman he'd ever loved. Of her wild red hair flowing down her back as Wilde smiled and pulled her close.

"Gemma is mine!"

"Bridget is mine!" The men announced the names at the same time and then looked at one another.

"Interesting." Ambrose laughed. "Say, I think I'll have another." He waved his glass at the proprietor and returned to his seat.

"Gemma? But I thought it was…" Anthony's voice trailed off, his chest suddenly tight. He had sent her a letter, told her that he wanted nothing more to do with her. That he could never love a woman he didn't trust… and she thought…

Anthony cursed. The room swayed… and he fell into blackness, hoping to stay there for eternity. For what point was there in living — when one wished to be dead?

Chapter One
En Garde

Four unfortunate weeks earlier

"Dance with her!" Cordelia ordered Anthony, poking him square in the chest with her gloved hand.

"Cordelia, you're making a scene!" He cursed and felt the heat of embarrassment spread down his neck. What he wouldn't do to be rid of his sister-in-law and her embarrassing taunts. She was just as bad as Ambrose.

"I swore I would revere the day I saw my brother blush!" Ambrose's solo applause brought Anthony a renewed sense of ill will toward his twin brother, which must have registered on his face. "Well done, my dear. Anthony looks quite put out."

"I assure you, I'm fine." Anthony cleared his throat to mask his indignation.

Just then Wilde approached the group. "Has he worked up his nerve yet, or are we still in the coaxing stage?"

Traitor.

"Still coaxing," Ambrose and Cordelia answered in unison. Ambrose gave his wife a wink and pulled her far too

1

close. Anthony knew they were happy, but must they flaunt it before him and the rest of society?

Anthony glanced toward the lady in question once more. She was lovely. Perhaps the finest he had seen in quite some time. Her dark red hair framed her fair face in delicate ringlets, and the blue of her gown set off her eyes like brilliant sapphires. He felt Ambrose watching him and turned back to his brother.

Ambrose's eyes held that dangerous look, as if a devious plan was forming in his mind as he spoke. "Say, Anthony?"

"What?" The crazed glint in his brother's eyes disturbed him, but he trained his own gaze on the girl by the plants again, feigning boredom, when boredom was truly the furthest thing from his mind. Kissing? Tangling his fingers in that glorious red mane? Pushing her deeper into the shadows of the hall? Those were his real thoughts.

"Would you agree that every Season you are approached by several women for little dalliances?" Ambrose asked.

"Yes." It would do no good to ignore his questions. He'd simply continue asking them until finally, in a fit of rage, Anthony would answer with a loud bellow, earning him haughty looks from society's patrons.

"Would you also agree that you're one of the most sought after bachelors in the *ton*?"

Devil take it, was he still talking?

Beside him, Wilde cursed. "I'll answer that for you. Just this morning in the park a girl cried when he picked up her fallen hat."

"Perfect," Ambrose said. "Do you believe you could make any woman fall in love with you then, Anthony? Or have you lost your touch?"

Oh, so that was what this was about. Anthony couldn't stop the grin from spreading across his lips. He did have an enviable touch when it came to the gentler sex.

"Not that it matters, but yes, I do believe that." Anthony

smoothed out his jacket with pride. He could have any woman eating out of his hand within minutes of an introduction. Yes, he was that good. His prowess had never once been disputed.

"Any girl?"

"To be certain." Anthony thought the line of questioning ridiculous. His brother knew his talent better than anyone else in the world.

Wilde appeared to be mumbling a prayer heavenward. Strange. Praying a fraction of Anthony's charms would be bestowed upon him, no doubt.

"And you're willing to wager you could accomplish this in say… four weeks?"

"Yes." Anthony nodded. This discussion was growing tiresome. The view was nice though. The girl's ruby lips were drawn into a tight pout. She turned her head to address someone over her shoulder. Was that a hint of fire in her eyes? Her apparent spirit intrigued him, and he found himself wishing his present conversation would end so he could obtain an introduction to his newest conquest.

"Shake my hand, Anthony," Ambrose ordered.

Anthony reached out and shook his hand. A sudden realization struck him. What had he just given his consent to? He cursed under his breath.

Ambrose grinned. "What was that?"

"Did I just agree to a bet?"

"Yes, and guess who I'm choosing." Ambrose rubbed his gloved hands together.

Anthony closed his eyes. "I don't want to guess. I want to go back in time and slap myself before I accepted the terms."

"Not possible. Do you see that girl over there? The one you've been salivating over for the past ten minutes while you handed over your life to me on a silver platter?"

"Son of a—" Anthony mumbled.

"You haven't called me that in ages!" Ambrose slapped him on the back. "Her. You must make her fall in love with you in four weeks' time. You have the devil's own fortune, so it shouldn't take any longer. Good luck!"

"Why do I feel like this is going to go terribly wrong?" Wilde muttered.

"Or," Cordelia said as she kissed Ambrose on the cheek, "it could go terribly right."

"Yes... yes, it could." Ambrose leaned down and scandalously kissed his wife full on the mouth. "After all, it's just a bet."

Why did they have to do that in public? Had they any idea how scandalous it was to kiss one's wife in public? On the mouth, no less? They might as well start stripping one another and — Anthony stopped his thoughts from going into dangerous territory.

Cordelia giggled, swatting at her husband with her reticule. "Who knows where it will lead?"

"Probably somewhere near the potted plants." He pointed as the lady in question stepped behind the ficus.

Anthony rolled his eyes in disgust and walked away. His brother's words faded as the great hall filled with music. It hardly seemed like a fair bet. The girl hadn't danced all evening. This would be a piece of cake for a devil-may-care charmer like himself.

And although he was a trifle irritated that Ambrose had used Anthony's woolgathering against him, he did love a challenge.

He smoothed his jacket and grabbed two flutes of champagne as a servant walked by. Tall, dark, handsome, and carrying a woman's favorite drink — who could resist him? Or the tiny bubbles that danced on the tongue? Naturally, she would know who he was when she clapped eyes on him, but introductions must be made.

He glanced to the side and noted the Dowager of Marseilles flipping her fan this way and that. Well, the little biddy knew everyone and everything; his instincts told him to go to her for an introduction.

"My lady." He bowed over the dowager's hand and grimaced when she tightened her grip and pulled him nearly into her lap. *Mustn't forget how many men she's single-handedly accosted.*

"What brings you over to the chaperones and elderly, my lord?" Dare he say it was her loveliness? The lady in question lifted a bushy brow and smiled revealing missing teeth. *Stop gaping!* he scolded himself. The last thing he needed was for her to think he was even a trifle interested in a dalliance.

He steeled himself against the elderly woman and smiled so brightly he was afraid the lady would expire on the spot. "I hoped to dance with you and your charge, or are you merely acquaintances?" He turned toward the glorious redhead and winked.

Either she was unmoved by his wink or she was blind. He smiled rakishly and noted the girl squeezing her eyes as if to inspect him. Blind it is. Pity.

"Ah, this is Lady Bridget. This is her first season, but I'm sure a man of your experience can tell these things. After all… you aren't known to go after the young ones. No." She patted his arm, allowing her jeweled hand to rest across his muscled forearm. "You enjoy a little spice and maturity. Do you not, my lord?"

Anthony imagined the look he gave her was similar to that of the looks foxes have when being hunted. Sweat moistened his brow, his fingers itched in his gloves, and he couldn't peel his eyes away from the lady's hand anymore than he could think of a way out of this predicament without obliging the elderly woman.

"My lord?" A sultry voice piped up to his right. Ah yes, the blind girl. Surely she could sense his distress even if she could not see it. "I wonder if you might get me some lemonade?"

Of course she wanted lemonade! Poor thing probably

couldn't manage on her own. "I'd be delighted." He offered an apology to the dowager, handed her a glass of champagne, and gently took the other lady's hand.

"My thanks," he breathed. "I wasn't sure if you could sense my desperate need of rescue." He threw back the contents of his own flute and grimaced.

She gave him a peculiar look, making him think she could see straight through him. What a silly notion! She was blind, after all.

Was it possible that when a person was blind he or she would also have trouble hearing? He cleared his throat and tried again. "How are you enjoying this fine evening, my lady? Allow me to compliment your gown. All others fade away when gazing upon such a beauty." He winked, more out of habit than anything, though he realized with irony that such a skilled wink was wasted on someone who couldn't appreciate it.

As they reached the lemonade table, he took a glass and placed it in her hand, careful to press it into fingers until she gripped it tightly. Seeming amused, she offered a curious smile and blinked several times before asking, "Are you foxed?"

Anthony laughed and shook his head. "Whatever would give you that idea?"

Her eyes darted from right to left several times before she answered. "You're acting like a complete fool! I wasn't saving you, by the way. I was saving myself. I want nothing more than to be free of that lady. Her only goal in mind is to match me up with the first bachelor to come my way."

"So, is she jotting down names then?" Anthony asked. "I do hope mine is on the top of that list."

"Oh, you're most assuredly on a list. Don't believe for a second it's mine though. I had half a mind to leave you with her just to see how such a rake could survive with an elderly woman. Pleasure her or flee? T'would be quite interesting, don't you think?"

"Apologies, my lady, but if you cannot see, how are you able to enjoy the entertainments you seem so wrapped up in?" Anthony winced at his own insensitivity, but better he come out with it now than later.

"Whatever do you mean?" Lady Bridget asked.

"Your eyes..." Anthony motioned in front of her face.

"What about them?"

Anthony felt himself flushing. "Devil take it! Why do women make things so difficult? Your eyes, they cannot see!"

"They cannot?" she repeated.

"Because you're blind." Anthony thought his statement quite helpful. He patted her hand as if to give her comfort.

Lady Bridget bit her lip and tilted her head. "Blind? How did you know?"

Anthony put down his lemonade — nasty stuff to begin with — and turned his devastating smile on her yet again. "I smiled."

"And that makes me blind?" Lady Bridget stepped closer to him, close enough for him to smell lilacs on her milky skin. Blast, how he wanted to reach out and touch her.

"Of course it does. You had no reaction whatsoever."

"Of all the hair-brained, egotistical notions!" Lady Bridget rolled her eyes and sipped her lemonade, casting a glance back over her shoulder toward the corner from whence she had come.

Anthony knew it couldn't be true, but she seemed bored with him if her stifled yawn and wandering gaze was any indication. If he was to win this bet, and so maintain bragging rights with his insufferable twin brother and their social circle, he had to hold her interest. He took another step toward her to regain her attention, reaching for her glass and fully intending to ask her to dance.

The step proved hazardous, however, and he felt his foot slip forward on something, causing his body to pitch backward and his arms and legs to flail in the air. The last thing Anthony remembered was a sharp pain slicing into the back of his head as he caught the edge of the refreshment table. Then darkness overtook him.

Chapter Two
A Worthy Opponent

Blind? Surely the man couldn't be serious. Granted, he was remarkably handsome with his soft wavy brown hair and his sage green eyes trimmed with a hint of gold. If she had a propensity for such things, Bridget supposed she could easily find herself lost in his gaze.

But she did not have the propensity.

And the man was an absolute cad.

Bridget could tell by that look in his eyes, the same haughty look she had seen in a hundred men these past few weeks, that he believed she would be an easy conquest. And she had every intention of dispelling his misconception of her the moment he asked her to dance.

But as he reached for her glass, the man lost his footing and fell, flailing to the ground. Bridget stifled a shocked laugh. *Pride goeth before a destruction*, she thought and slipped away to allow enough room for others to see to the viscount's injury.

****

The haze dissipated slowly as if he were returning from some sort of dream filled with a dashing redhead. On second thought, it was a nightmare, for his eyes made out the fuzzy image of Wilde crouched above him. The man's lips were moving, but whatever words issuing forth from him made no sense. Slowly Anthony's other senses came into focus, and confusion set in. What had happened?

"Say something, man!" Wilde was shouting in his face.

"Your breath… is reminiscent of a fire breathing dragon, Wilde. Please direct it elsewhere," Anthony whispered in a husky voice.

Wilde rocked back on his heels, his face reddened with irritation. Behind him Ambrose laughed.

"I'd say he's recovered," his brother announced.

Anthony sat up slowly. His head throbbed, so he reached a tremulous hand to the lump now protruding from the back of his skull. It was dry. No blood. At least he hadn't spilled his innards in front of the lady. Nothing makes a woman more likely to swoon than a man projecting blood on her person.

The events leading to his present state began to swirl back through his mind. Lady Bridget. To where had she disappeared? Were they not just in conversation? Wasn't she concerned for his welfare? Devil take it! A woman should know her place! She should help a man when he… had a tumble.

He cast a pensive glance around the room to search for her, but there were too many people crowding about him.

The music started up again, dispersing the concerned spectators.

Ambrose offered his hand. "Can you stand, brother?" A mischievous grin taunted Anthony from his twin's face.

"I believe so. What the devil happened?" He allowed his brother to assist him. Beside him, Wilde chuckled with a hand covering his mouth.

"You slipped on a strawberry." He pointed to the mashed

offending fruit. "Fortunately, it appears the fiend got the worst of it."

"I hate blasted strawberries, of course that would be the culprit." Anthony made a move to kick the fruit but stopped his childish notion when his brother piped up.

"I dare say you made quite the impression on the young lady," Ambrose added, gesturing back to the corner where she sat once again. "She made short work of excusing herself from your company. Naturally, she waited until after you were unconscious, which I find most gracious. Pray tell, did you find yourself out of your depth?"

"Four weeks, Ambrose. This is only the first night." Anthony seethed beneath the surface. A glimmer of doubt turned his stomach. He hoped this incident was not indicative of how the next four weeks would play out.

"I do hope your form improves, for your sake — and hers," Ambrose said.

So do I. Oh, so do I, Anthony thought and rubbed the sensitive lump on the back of his head once more, finally resting his gaze on the lady in question. This could prove more difficult than he originally anticipated.

Dare he make another move to speak to the girl? Her back was now facing him. Surely she was concerned! Anthony was unable to comprehend a woman who would not only watch a man fall, but also not wait to see that he was uninjured. Usually women tripped him on purpose in hopes that he would fall into their arms and be forced into marriage! It was the one reason he vigilantly looked to his feet when walking down darkened hallways. Fortunately for him, women took it as a sign of humility. Truly, it worked out perfectly.

He squinted in her direction, willing her to turn around. But after a horrifying three minutes he relented and glanced back toward the opposite side of the room, assuming Wilde and Ambrose would have returned to their usual posts.

Instead he came face to face with both men. Smiles plastered on their irritating lips and arms crossed. Anthony had the sudden urge to shoot them both for their mockery.

"Move aside," Anthony grumbled, pushing past them. He let out a string of expletives when he noticed they were following him.

"Oh, Anthony, darling!" Lady Burnside hollered at him.

Cursing again, he turned to his side. "Ah, my lady, how does the evening fare?"

She moved close enough for him to decipher that she had consumed her fair share of roasted pig and sherry and whispered, "It could be better, if you gain my meaning."

Saints alive, the woman was strong. Her grip tightened on his forearm. Truly, he wished to be anywhere but here. Why was it that every elderly lady in the room, especially the married ones, propositioned him?

Every Season.

And every Season, Anthony rejected the poor women and prayed for temporary blindness to conveniently strike him every time a lady as notorious as Lady Burnside walked in the room. Oh, she was an attractive lady, but the dresses she wore were indecent. And when one doesn't necessarily fit into said dresses, well... it should be said that Anthony had trouble imagining how he could escape a tryst with the woman without being smothered. That thought alone kept him awake at night.

"My lady, it seems I've taken ill," Anthony apologized.

"Ill?" Wilde said from behind him.

"Yes," Anthony confirmed. "I took a slight fall."

Ambrose coughed wildly behind him.

"And," Anthony continued. "I need to nurse my—"

"Pride?" Ambrose offered.

"As well as other parts of his anatomy," Wilde chimed in cheerfully.

Lady Burnside grinned. "Nurse, you say? Oh dear me. In

that case, you have happened in the right direction, my lord! You are in luck, for I can nurse you back to health!"

"How gracious," Wilde said.

"Yes." Ambrose coughed again. "You are a saint among sinners, my lady."

"I do try," she agreed. "Now how shall I help?"

Anthony hated lying — hated being mocked by his brother, and thought to himself that it couldn't get any worse — and then...

"Aunt?" Lady Bridget approached.

Anthony inwardly cursed. He must have done something horribly offensive for God to allow him to be embarrassed twice within the same hour in front of the same beautiful girl he was supposed to be impressing.

"Ah, Bridget, my girl! I cannot attend to you just now. I have been given the task of nursing Viscount Maddox back to health! Did you know the poor gentleman was injured?"

Bridget tilted her head and offered a sly smile. "No, Aunt. Perhaps I was stricken with a momentary blindness. For although I heard a scuffle, I was unable to ascertain what unfortunate accident transpired. Whatever happened, my lord?"

Anthony glared. "Son of a—"

"Saint!" Wilde blurted. "You are such a saint, my lady, for helping Lord Maddox, but I believe the best medicine will be for us to see him home for a much needed respite."

"Are you sure?" Lady Burnside seemed disappointed. Anthony, however, couldn't decipher between his own aggravation with the Lady Bridget's lack of interest and his pure fear of her aunt's advances.

"Positive." Ambrose winked. "Ladies, it has been a pleasure." With a curt bow, Ambrose motioned for Anthony to follow. He had no choice but to bow to both women and pray his face wouldn't give way to the frustration he felt at Bridget's comment. The little minx had done it on purpose!

"Oh, Viscount Maddox?" Bridget called out as he turned to leave.

Perhaps she did care. She was only jesting; he really should give her a chance, after all—

"Be sure to sleep on your side."

Anthony's nostrils flared and he took a step back in her direction. "Now see here—"

"Good night to you, ladies." Wilde pushed Anthony in front of him, making it impossible to give the girl a good set down.

****

Bridget could feel the smug grin creasing her lips as she stared after the gentlemen's retreat. The man would be nursing more than a bruised head this evening. She'd made sure of that.

After doing her best to avoid attention from the gentlemen at the party, the last thing she needed was the Benson twins turning her into their own personal Pygmalion project. She hoped her interaction with Lord Maddox had gone unnoticed by the rest of the bachelors in attendance.

She had promised her aunt she would participate in a Season, but she had no intention of participating in the marriage mart. There were far too many other worthy aspirations in life. Yes, even for a woman. Art, literature, politics, writing. Bridget longed for the liberty to follow her own desired pursuits.

Most men expected women to sit at home and work on their needlework, or perhaps play the piano, or God forbid, visit other women who love nothing more than to gossip. She'd watched her mother's light slowly fade as a child. Her parents had once seemed so happy, and then suddenly they weren't. Memories of her mother reading to her and then hiding the same books she was reading replayed in Bridget's mind, how her parents would fight when her father was again disappointed that her mother had been a bad hostess, or not ordered enough wine for the parties they had.

Bridget wanted none of it. To have a man dictate her life, her happiness, was not only unfair but ridiculous. She would rather die a spinster. At least as a spinster she could pursue writing. Her true passion. Perhaps *Pride and Prejudice* was to blame; after all, the women in that book had strong opinions of their own. What would it be like to write such a tale? She sighed longingly.

Feeling as though she was being watched, Bridget whipped around and noticed the heat of her aunt's glare falling heavy on her. She waited for the inevitable derision. Aunt Latissia had promised Bridget's grandmother she would see to a proper Season. And that meant proposals. Proposals enough to have an option for an acceptable match. Never mind that Aunt Latissia would be championing her own cause along with her. The woman's shameless advances on the young men of the *ton* were mortifying to say the least.

"Bridget," her aunt began. "Did you have words with Lord Maddox earlier? He seemed anxious to get away from you. What did you do?"

Fighting an overwhelming urge to roll her eyes and suggest the root of his anxiety could be her aunt's salivating over him like a dog in heat, Bridget inhaled slowly and pretended to consider the question.

"I can't think of a single thing that could have caused such a reaction, Aunt. We had such a pleasant conversation, and he helped me to some lemonade."

"You're up to something, girl. Your grandmother made me promise to find you a husband. And after all she did for you after your mother's death — taking you in and caring for you — the least you can do is oblige the old woman by encouraging the gentlemen to seek your hand. Gratefulness is a Fruit of the Spirit. You'll do well to practice it."

"Yes, Aunt." Bridget lowered her head in feigned repentance, hoping it would prompt a dismissal and the end of the lecture. Though the argument was riddled with theological inaccuracy, to make that point would simply prolong the interaction.

"Now run along and dance with someone."

Bridget glanced back to her aunt to find the woman had already spotted her next quarry and was licking her lips and pinching her cheeks. With a shallow curtsy, Bridget made a quick escape back to the corner near the plants.

One dance. That was all she had to do to fulfill her aunt's instructions. It should be someone harmless. She glanced around the room for a suitable partner.

Sir Bryan. Yes, he would do.

The Lady Cristina, his intended, had left town for a few days for her grandfather's funeral, and Sir Bryan had been moping about all evening as if at sixes and sevens. A perfect partner.

With one flash of her fan, she caught his attention and waved him over. No one would notice if she danced with him. Yes, he would do quite nicely.

Chapter Three
Parry and Riposte

"Truly you can't fault Anthony for his glaring stupidity. After all, he cannot help being born with such a handicap. Think how it must affect him," Wilde said.

Ambrose lifted his snifter of brandy. "Agreed."

"Born with stupidity?" Anthony raged. He had been sitting in the corner stewing since daybreak over that wretched strawberry while Ambrose and Wilde pretended to be helpful.

"One can hardly fault the strawberry," Ambrose argued further. "I'm wholly convinced the blame rests with Mother. If she would have merely eaten more strawberries, Anthony wouldn't find the fruit so offensive, and that same fruit wouldn't have skittered about his boots seeking revenge."

"Fruit doesn't seek revenge, you idiot." Anthony felt the need to defend himself.

They ignored him.

"Has he ever tried a strawberry?" Wilde sounded genuinely curious.

"Anthony refuses to try things more than once. Says it's a

waste of his time. Isn't that so, brother?"

"Yes, but—"

Wilde shook his head. "Does that same sensibility apply to wooing young ladies? Sounds silly to me. Perseverance is a virtue, my friend. It would be a considerable error in Anthony's judgment to follow that creed. For he already tried to beguile the girl once, and look where it got him."

They shot sympathetic looks his way. He half expected the men to bow their heads in reverence.

"'Tis merely a bruised—"

"Ego?" Wilde offered.

"Bum?" Ambrose suggested.

"I'm going home," Anthony announced, gritting his teeth against the pain in his backside as he rose from his seat and hobbled to the study door. "And if I find any sort of strawberry, or heaven forbid, Lady Burnside in my room when I get there, there will be the devil to pay, I assure you."

"Couldn't really fight her off in his present condition though." Ambrose elbowed Wilde.

"Yes," Wilde agreed. "Wouldn't be fair for us to do such a thing in his weakened state."

"Good afternoon!"

It had been one whole day, and Anthony still walked with a limp. It hurt to stretch, to breathe — basically, it hurt to exist. Not that he wanted to let on to any of his acquaintances that he was suffering so.

It was all Lady Bridget's fault. The only comfort he found was in imagining what would have happened had he avoided that cursed strawberry.

Lush red lips would have firmly pressed against his in a hot fervor of exotic bliss. Unfortunately, when he thought of her lush red lips, his mind immediately conjured up the image of a lush red strawberry, making his backside throb with pain once more.

How was he to impress the girl? He couldn't dance

without wanting to cry out. No telling how many women would flock if they knew he was injured. He'd be married by the week's end. The women of the *ton* seemed to sense weakness and attack with a fervor like none other. Anthony often imagined men as defenseless zebras and the women as preying lions. And at this point in his life, he was most definitely the vulnerable baby zebra. He wouldn't stand a chance. Being devoured was not on the top of his list for the day, nor was sitting and listening to Wilde and Ambrose laugh at his expense.

The soreness in his back made walking home look much more comfortable than riding in a jostling curricle, so he rounded the corner of the block and embarked for home, taking slow stiff strides.

As he limped, Anthony considered his strategies. He had only four weeks. And what seemed like ample time yesterday as he admired the lady from a distance, now after their introduction appeared as a wildfire fast on his heels. How is it that out of the entire flock of fresh debutantes, Ambrose had selected the only lady who would despise him simply by virtue of his confidence? The only one who would put up a fight?

He pushed the thoughts of doubt from his mind. After all, he was Anthony Benson, Viscount Maddox. His prowess with the ladies was the stuff of legends, and a challenge like this one would only serve to sharpen his skills.

If there were some way he could determine which social events Lady Bridget would be attending for the next four weeks without raising suspicion, he could tailor his own appearances to mimic hers, and so create a variety of *coincidental* meetings. If nothing else, the mere familiarity of seeing him everywhere might begin to wear down her defenses. And certainly, the regular exposure to his charms alone would do her in.

Yes. Anthony was feeling better already — a slight

swagger returned to his gait. He inhaled deeply of the sweet afternoon air and glanced about the street to see who was about.

A young lady walking a small dog, followed closely by her lady's maid, who carried the parasol, caught his eye. It was the lady who had been haunting his thoughts. Anthony was sure of it. How fortuitous! His plans need not wait until later.

He stepped into the street without thinking and narrowly missed being rundown by a speeding hack. His heart leapt into his throat, forcing him to jump backward to the cobblestone walkway. Naturally, the sudden jolt caused him to lose his footing, and he skittered to the ground, landing firmly on his already damaged backside.

The heat of humiliation rose to his face. With haste he stood again and brushed the street dust from his breeches. It wouldn't do to have the lady witness him in distress again so soon. A quick glance in her direction assured him she hadn't noticed his misfortune, so he attempted again to cross, this time waiting for the traffic to pass before venturing into the street. Pain and indignation shot through him with each step.

He decided on a rear attack and came first upon the lady's maid, who startled when he reached to take the parasol from her. Anthony gestured with a finger to his lips for her to keep the secret, and the servant girl cast a shy smile in his direction and nodded, falling back a few paces but not before winking an invitation in his direction. At least he still had his touch. Or so he thought, until he reached Bridget's side and she began speaking.

"You are quite accident prone, are you not, my lord?"

"Whatever do you mean?" He lied through his teeth and ventured a glance at his breeches for any hint of dust remnants.

The girl refused to look in his direction. "You took another tumble, did you not? Or were you merely playing a game with the carriages, living dangerously as the great

Viscount Maddox is known for doing?"

Ignoring her stab at his reputation, he let out a whistle. "My, my, so you do pay attention to my reputation as well as other things. Tell me, do you also know my favorite color and choice of horseflesh?"

Lady Bridget froze and gave him a glare so horrendously pointed that he was sure he would go up in flames.

"Are you always this prideful?"

For a lack of a better answer, he nodded, gracing her with the full force of his smile. "Tell me," he said, gaining strength from her obvious fidgeting. "Have you always been afraid of a man's attention, or is this fear only bestowed upon those as lucky as myself?"

"A man's attention?" she repeated with a laugh. "Do tell me when we come upon a man, for I would like to see what a real one looks like up close. Good day, my lord."

Mouth agape, Anthony stared as she did a quick curtsy and walked by him. He grabbed the maid's arm as she hurried to catch up to her mistress. "Is she going out tonight?"

The maid's complexion took on a rosy hue. "Yes, my lord. To the Brampton dinner party," she answered in a whisper.

He winked and handed her the parasol, allowing her to be on her way. No chance the girl would reject him twice in one day. Surely she could not be so heartless!

Chapter Four
Rejection is Such Sweet Sorrow

Not even her afternoon walk was sacred anymore. Lord Maddox was an exasperating man — so brazen and petulant in his vanity. Bridget exhaled sharply and shook her head to knock loose the thoughts of the infuriating rogue. She didn't wish to think of him at all. Because unfortunately when she thought of him, it was either grand irritation that plagued her mind, or the undeniable fact that he was the most beautiful man she had ever seen. And for some reason, he wanted her attention. Fighting the urge to smile at the thought, she focused once again on her walk, on clearing her head, and perhaps yes, plotting her next book. Perhaps the main character would slip on a strawberry.

She snorted with disdain. Everything she had heard of the viscount had only served to form an ill opinion of him, regardless of how high in regard the whole of the *ton* held him and his brother. Between the two of them, Lord Maddox was the least respectable. He was known to entertain occasional dalliances with the widows and charm his way through the *ton* with that blasted smile on his face. All he needed to do was flash a devastating grin in the general direction of the female population and swoons surely followed.

Well, she was not going to be another one of his conquests. In fact, she found the notion so repulsive that when her heart fluttered in his presence and her breath grew ragged, she attributed it to a sickness brought on by his masculine scent.

Impossible that her body reacted to him that strongly, she refused to acknowledge it. The man had no shame. And she had better things to occupy her thoughts. Again she concentrated on her newest work. A novel. And again, his face flashed in her mind. He would be the perfect Mr. Darcy. His strong form and rakish smile.

Still, it was pleasing to see him humbled twice in two days. A mischievous smirk curled her lips at the memory of Lord Maddox knocked squarely on his rear. And on a public street. Yes, that image was sure to bring her hours of good humor for the weeks to come as she endured the rest of the wretched London Season. Her walk suddenly took a turn for the better, for every time she thought of the handsome viscount, she remembered his accidents and immediately lost the attraction she held for him. At least, that's what she told herself to believe when her thoughts turned dangerous.

****

Already Bridget was relieved her aunt had taken ill that afternoon. Since she was unable to accompany her to the dinner party, Bridget had come with her dear friend Gemma Reynolds. The freedom from her aunt's heavy-handed scrutiny of Bridget's every move, as well as the lack of formal dancing, gave Bridget liberty to avoid hiding in corners from unwelcome attempts at forcing her to participate.

She sat chatting with Gemma and her brother, waiting for the entertainments to begin. Gemma was slated to play the pianoforte later this evening after dinner, a talent that escaped Bridget, but she did enjoy listening to her friend's mastery of the instrument.

Bridget had known Gemma for years. Many times they had been mistaken for sisters, because their hair was the same brilliant shade of crimson — though Bridget had often wished she could trade her wild insubordinate curls for a satin smooth mane like Gemma's.

Ever since her mother's death and Bridget had come to live with her father's family in London — though the man himself had abandoned both Bridget and her mother when she was but a child — Gemma and Bridget had been in constant company and loved one another like sisters. But Gemma's aspirations were toward marriage nowadays, so her subjects of choice in conversation held little interest for Bridget.

Therefore it was little wonder that Bridget was only half-listening to the discussion of the announced betrothal between Count Belvedere and Miss Violet Jasper when her friend stopped talking mid-sentence and anchored her gaze on the archway behind Bridget.

"Sweet heavens... sin just walked through the door," Gemma whispered in ironic reverence. Her head tilted to the side, a feminine sigh escaped her lips, and Bridget could have sworn her friend actually began to tear up.

As Bridget twisted in her chair to see what was affecting her friend so, Gemma rested a hand on Bridget's to stay her, stopping her from turning wholly around.

And something in Gemma's urgency caused Bridget to stiffen in purest dread, when her friend added, "Oh! I may swoon! He's approaching us!"

"The devil you say!"

"He comes at this very moment!" Gemma clenched her hands in her lap and began to visibly shake.

If the sudden chill prickling along her spine was any indication, Bridget was certain that the *sin* rendering her friend paralyzed at this moment was none other than Viscount Maddox, and he stood directly behind her, with his usual beautiful smile spread across his smug face. How did he know she would be here? Well, she wasn't going to gift him the satisfaction of knowing she could sense his presence. That would be just what he wanted. Drat her arms for producing chills, and curse her stomach for dropping to her knees!

"Holy Moses, no man should have a smile like that," Gemma said just under her breath.

Bridget rolled her eyes, but had to grudgingly agree. His smile could melt the ice off a polar bear's tail.

"Lady Bridget, a word?"

Gemma's mouth gaped, betraying her shock.

Bridget stood before turning around, giving herself time to steel her nerves against the onslaught of his overwhelming male ego. At least he came by it honestly. The viscount truly was carved like a Greek god. But she had no intention of allowing it to affect her. She has other interests — other pursuits, and —

"My buttons, they make a handsome couple," Gemma's brother said loud enough for all to hear. Gemma jabbed him in the ribs with a well-placed elbow.

"Ah, Lord Maddox. Speak of the devil and he appears — what an unlikely surprise."

"You were speaking of me?" His beguiling smile stretched wider across his marble features.

"Hmm… if I recall correctly, we spoke of sin, and yes, I believe the devil was mentioned." His smile waned to its usual irritating level. The golden corona of his brilliant green eyes seemed to catch the candlelight and sparkle at her. No. Bridget wouldn't let him convince her. She was no trophy to be won. Why wouldn't he just leave her alone? *Think about your mother crying! Think about your parents' marriage crumbling and your mother dying of a broken heart. Think of those things!*

As if on cue, Sir Wilde interjected with genuine pleasure,

"Lady Gemma! It has been an age!" He brushed past the viscount to address the lady's hand. "Tell me, where have you been keeping yourself?"

Gemma seemed to blush to the very roots of her dark red hair. He tucked her hand under his arm and led her to the refreshment table, chattering all the while.

Bridget shook her head slightly as the pair disappeared around the corner without so much as batting an eyelash in farewell. Behind them, Gemma's traitor of a brother followed close, as if he didn't trust Sir Wilde a stone's throw away with his sister.

This left Bridget quite alone in the salon. Quite alone with Lord Maddox.

The man took a seat beside where Bridget stood and gestured to her to do the same. As she lowered herself into the chair, he leaned in ever so close and turned that sinful smile on her. Suddenly overheated and beyond irritation, she began to fan herself, trying desperately to appear nonchalant when the temptation to lean forward and smell him was overwhelming.

"You asked for a word, my lord. How may I be of help to you this evening? Perhaps a lesson or two on how to walk about the public streets without being trampled by passing carriages? Or possible strategies to avoid dangerous fruit attacks?" Bridget offered him what she hoped was her most innocent expression. "Truly, I aim only to please."

"It seems I've found my match. I do so love a challenge."

"I'm not participating in said challenge, nor am I like every other girl who would think nothing of selling her own grandmother in order to receive one of your smiles."

"Truly? You wouldn't even sell a dress? An irritating sibling?"

"Not a sibling, and certainly not my soul."

"Truly, you have a rapier sharp wit, my lady. Pray tell, how do you do it?"

"I read, my lord," she replied. "I daresay none of the

women of your prior acquaintance can boast such."

"Indeed," he said, eyeing her with a hint of doubt in his own charms. That ought to finish him. A couple of well placed poisoned darts in his more than adequate ego and he would be but a memory of this tedious night. Dare she drive the nail home?

"Perhaps the talent eludes even you, my lord."

A shallow, sickly smile spread over his lips. Yes, she was getting to him.

"You may think of me as you please, my lady." His gaze drifted past her searching for his comrade who had disappeared as though seeking a swift escape. Good. The desired effect. No reason to postpone the inevitable. Men leave. The arrogant ones leave sooner. It was a simple matter of time. At least it was for her father.

"You presume much, my lord. For when this conversation is at an end, I will not think of you at all." His golden-crested emerald eyes flashed the briefest betrayal of his pain. Bridget knew she had said too much, and an icy twinge of guilt spread from the pit of her stomach to her extremities. Her ears burned, and she knew without doubt they were a fiery beacon of her regret. For a moment, Bridget was glad of her scarlet tresses, since they would do much to camouflage her vibrant ears.

She tore her gaze from his face, glanced toward the nearby doors, and waited for him to excuse himself.

"If that is the case," he said, a hint of amusement dancing in his deep, rich voice, "We shall simply continue this conversation for eternity."

****

Anthony felt his lips curl into a smile as his point was made. Lady Bridget shut her fan with a click and glared.

"An eternity is quite a long time to fill with enough topics worthy of discussion, my lord. For my part, I don't wish to insult you by allowing any more opportunities for you to make a complete fool of yourself. Good evening, my lord." She bestowed a sweet mocking smile, stood, and left him.

Alone.

Feeling quite ridiculous.

That went well. Anthony shook his head to clear the cloud of confusion just as Wilde stumbled back into the salon.

"Whatever is the matter with you? You look like you've seen a ghost, Anthony. You're as white as a sheet."

"I'm going to lose," Anthony admitted with a curse. There had to be something strong to drink close at hand. His gaze scanned the room for any sort of beverage to numb his humiliation and cursed attraction to that wretched girl.

Wilde grinned like the fool he was and slapped Anthony on the back. "Cheer up! It can't be that bad!"

"It is…"

"What?" Wilde looked confused.

"That bad," Anthony confirmed.

"What were we discussing again?" Wilde stared at the door expectantly.

"Are you listening to me at all?" Anthony asked. The least Wilde could do was give him his undivided attention in this moment of his greatest need. "I need advice, support." God forbid, he was going to say the one thing he'd never uttered aloud. "I need…" *Oh, foul word of the weak!* "…help," he finished, hanging his head in defeat.

"Well, the way I see it, most people don't use kelp in any sort of recipe anymore. Though I'll try to find some for you, if you truly need it. Is it for stomach ache?"

"What the devil are you talking about?" Anthony took a good hard look at his friend. His very flushed and nervous-looking friend. "I said *help,* you idiot, not *kelp.* What in the name of Hades would I use kelp for?"

"I thought it was an odd request. My humblest apology,

my lord," Wilde mumbled, his eyes still trained on the door.

My lord? Perfect. His friend was going to be no help whatsoever. Anthony made a move to leave, but Wilde stopped him.

"Say I have a friend..." Wilde started.

Merciful heavens above. Anthony felt like being selfish. He had problems of his own. Gargantuan problems. He didn't have time for this! "I used to have many friends, until they started ignoring my pleas for help."

"So this friend..." Wilde continued. "He wants to impress a certain lady."

"Ah, it's often about a lady."

"How—" Wilde shifted, finally taking his attention off the door. "That is to say, when might it be appropriate to — bestow a kiss?"

"Bestow a...? For the love of—"

"I know you have experience in the matter. And Ambrose would only laugh at me. Whereas you might explain it to me in terms I can comprehend," Wilde said, cutting off Anthony's curse.

Guilt washed over him as he glanced at his nervous friend. Wilde hadn't a nervous bone in his body! What the devil was bothering him? Must be some woman to have him worked up thus. Blast! Wilde's reputation was no different than Anthony's and his brother's. His current behavior made no sense. It was odd to see him acting like such a nervous schoolboy.

Anthony sat back down with a heavy sigh of resignation. "Is this particular lady... skittish?"

"She's the proper sort, yes..." Wilde smiled.

Anthony fought the urge to close his eyes in exasperation. "Does this lady have any experience with men?"

Wilde's eyes sparked to life. "If she does, I'll kill them, every last one! I'll challenge them each in turn to a duel to the death, and—"

"Easy, man. It was merely a question."

Wilde nodded in understanding, his brown eyes still aflame with indignation at the suggestion.

"For everyone's sake, let us assume she is inexperienced. The best way to bestow a first kiss upon a woman is to take her by surprise."

"Like when hunting for foxes?" Wilde offered.

"Yes, an excellent analogy. That is, your lips would be the shot, and perhaps the woman, the fox."

"So I sneak up on her?" Wilde asked.

Anthony cursed and ran his fingers through his hair. He really was in no position to be giving out advice, especially about that of the opposite sex. Currently, he was having trouble of his own coaxing a certain woman to so much as smile at him, while also avoiding the stinging daggers of her cunning words.

"Don't scare her, Wilde. Simply grab her and kiss her—"

"Grab her? How?" Wilde was painfully out of his element. So much in fact, that Anthony took pity on him and decided to truly show his friend what he meant. With a quick glance to see if anyone might intrude, Anthony turned toward his lovesick friend.

"Like this." Anthony placed his hands on Wilde's shoulders, giving them a firm shake. "Now, you need to show this woman that you are firm, but gentle at the same time. When she gazes upon you..." Wilde batted his eyelashes at him. *Oh sweet heavens, Ambrose must never get wind of this.* "Wilde, please... do you want me to show you or not? I do have other more pressing concerns."

"I'm sorry. Please continue," he answered with a nervous chortle.

"Fine. Now, when she gazes upon you, tilt your head to the side and kiss her cheek."

"Her cheek? But I want to kiss—"

"It's safe to assume I know what you want to kiss, but

you must take care not to scare her at the first. If she is receptive, then you kiss the other cheek."

"And if she isn't receptive?"

"If she isn't, I daresay she'll plant something on your cheek you won't soon forget."

Wilde appeared thoughtful. "But why not the lips?" he asked after a long moment.

"Consider it, Wilde. Do you run at the fox shooting like a madman?"

He shook his head.

"Of course not. Hunting foxes is a sport of finesse. An art form." Anthony patted his friend's shoulder. "You coax the fox from its den. Much the same way you coax the woman. You draw her to you, and then you go in for the kill."

"So I kiss her after she warms to me?"

"By Jove, I think you've got it." *Finally.* Anthony smiled. Truly it was a brilliant analogy if he did say so himself.

"And then she'll be receptive?" Wilde asked hopefully.

A strange thought suddenly occurred to Anthony. "Colin, why are you asking me this? Surely you have done this before..." Anthony's hands lingered on Wilde's shoulders just as Ambrose strode through the door.

With a jerk, Anthony dropped his hands to his sides, but it was too late. Ambrose's mocking smile stretched to his ears. He crossed his arms and leaned against the wall. "I do hope I'm not intruding, but a little bird told me some information I thought might help you in your quest for Lady Bridget's affection. Of course, I'm only too happy to wait for you to finish wooing Wilde."

"I was not wooing Wilde," Anthony argued.

Wilde, the traitorous son of a Frenchman, slipped back into his old humor and threw Anthony to the wolves. "He was demonstrating how to properly kiss a woman — or was that how to trap one, Anthony?"

Ambrose's eyes widened and he began to choke and

laugh at the same time. "By all means, continue!"

"We are done here," Anthony said through clenched teeth. "You said something about *helpful* information, I believe."

Wilde grinned. "Yes, I do recall our dear friend begging for help only moments ago."

"So now you get it right?" Anthony muttered. "Brilliant."

"Haven't heard him utter that word since he was three." Ambrose scoffed and took a seat. "It appears you have a long journey ahead of you, brother. Your little woman has quite the story, it seems. Although some of it is quite blotchy considering my sources were conveniently foxed during the telling of it."

"A likely story," Anthony remarked.

Ambrose adjusted his coattails to take a seat. "I don't think you'll find this encouraging, but I feel the need to share nonetheless."

Anthony leaned back in his seat. "Well, get on with it."

"The lady appears to have had a bad sort of upbringing. Her father left her mother and herself when she was but ten years of age — old enough to know what was happening, but too young to understand why. They were destitute and often relied on the church for charity in order to make it through the colder months."

"What kind of fool leaves his wife and child?" Anthony was alarmed with the idea of it all.

"A man in love with his own pursuits. And from what I've heard, he had many."

"Fool... What else?"

Ambrose took a swig of Wilde's whiskey. "The poor little girl was left to care for her mother all alone, and the woman died in her daughter's arms not two years after the dirty philanderer left them."

Anthony felt the sudden urge to hunt the man down and kill him with his bare hands, preferably in a slow savage manner. "How did she come to be under the protection of her extended family?"

Ambrose shook his head. "Her grandmother, whom we have yet to see, the Dowager Countess of Darlingshire, hasn't stepped foot in society since her husband's death. Leaving the task of the girl's debut to…"

"Lady Burnside," Anthony finished, shuddering as the thought swirled around in his head.

"Correct." Ambrose shared in the shudder. "It seems the only objective of Lady Bridget's family is to see her married off."

"Yes, and that boded so well for her mother." Anthony was sickened to his very core. "How could they be so insensitive to the young girl's needs? Any child would scoff at the Season or an arranged marriage, all things considered."

"So you see why this makes your task difficult?" Ambrose asked.

Anthony shrugged. "Nigh impossible. But I find the information useful nonetheless."

Wilde blanched. "So you mean to put the girl through this silly bet in order to appease your own pride?"

"I never lose." Anthony shrugged, though inside his stomach churned in protest. He wouldn't lose, but he would never put an innocent lady through such hardship. The situation called for a different strategy. Another means to an end.

Wilde glowered at him with a heartless vengeance, while Ambrose threw back the contents of his glass.

"If you're sure you wish to proceed, brother…"

"Of course." Anthony managed to laugh. "Tis a silly bet. Nothing more, am I right? Now let us off to dinner."

****

It was by sheer luck that Anthony managed to secure a

seat next to Lady Bridget. All intentions were selfless, for he meant to put her at ease as well as apologize. That is, before the minx stabbed him with her fork... twice. Nevermind that they were eating soup. But he took it in stride and apologized for his clumsy hands being in the wrong place at the wrong time. Her obvious shock made it all worth it.

Now, the rub. How was he to apologize yet still have her participate in this farce so he could save face in front of his brother and Wilde, who were at this very moment both watching the entertainments from the opposite end of the table?

"I do apologize for my behavior," Anthony said, reaching for his wine. "It isn't often those words flow freely from my lips, so I beg you to record them in your mind."

Lady Bridget laughed then coughed. "Yes, I'll be sure to remember them the next time you offend, my lord."

"And there will be other times, I assure you." Anthony added. "After all, I'm a rogue and a flirt. Truly the worst sort of gentleman."

"Finally something we agree upon."

"Yes, and I have something else to confess. Though I ask you won't judge me too harshly."

Her hand stilled on the stem of her wine glass.

"I don't mean to be so taken with you. Clearly, it's your fault."

She fumbled, nearly tipping the wine glass over. "My fault?"

"But of course." He shook his head and gave her a look of pure innocence. "If you would not have flaunted that red hair, we would not now be in this predicament."

"Flaunted my red hair?" Her eyes widened.

Anthony shrugged. "Everyone knows I prefer redheads. Surely you knew that when you glanced in my direction last evening."

"I did nothing of the sort—"

"It is of no consequence." He waved her off. "For if your hair hadn't done it, your eyes surely would have."

"Whatever is the matter with my eyes?"

"Nothing." He swallowed and looked at her direct, knowing it was improper to be so clearly interested. "That's the blasted problem. Nothing is wrong with you. Absolutely nothing, and I find myself perplexed as to how to gain your attention — short of injuring myself, stepping in front of moving carriages, or putting my foot in my mouth. So, I do apologize, truly."

"I accept your apology as long as you understand I still think you a reckless rogue without a care for another soul in the world."

Anthony let out a hearty laugh. "Oh, I'm still that, and I beg you never to forget it, my lady." He lifted his glass in her direction as her eyes tightened into tiny slits.

****

Bridget was dumbfounded. He was being kind — still arrogant, but in an almost appealing way that made her stomach do flip flops and her heart pound against her chest even more so than before. Wanting to scream, she closed her eyes instead and focused on her breathing. What game was he playing? She hadn't done anything except insult him.

Whatever his game was, it would be so much easier to continue to give him the cut if he remained his haughty, supercilious self. Lord Maddox was a cockscomb. It made things simple for her. And she didn't want that to change.

By the time dinner was over, Lord Maddox was very nearly likeable. And Bridget's hands were clenched so hard within her lap that she was convinced she was suffering from blood loss. He was impossible to ignore when he was arrogant, and even more so when he winked with that rakish air that turned her knees to jelly.

The entire company retired to the salon to enjoy the evening's entertainments. Bridget turned to wait for Gemma, but she had already accepted Sir Wilde's escort and was leaving Bridget behind without so much as a second look. As dejection set in from the abandonment, Bridget began to make her own way into the salon. She didn't notice Lord Maddox waiting for her by the door until she nearly collided with him.

He lifted his elbow to her with an intoxicating smile. "May I escort you, my lady?"

She was reluctant to accept and hesitated for a moment before taking his arm. "If you think you can manage keeping us both on our feet," she said with a hint of irony. In a display of unenthusiastic resolve, she linked her arm with his and allowed Lord Maddox to guide her into the salon.

It was not a large party, so there were still a few seats left in the room when they entered. Lord Maddox led Bridget to a wingback on the far side from the pianoforte, and stood behind her as she sat.

Gemma was the first to play. Bridget had, of course, heard her friend play many times and knew her to be a talented musician. Bridget had no such talent, so she slowly rose from her seat and moved to the back of the room in hopes that no one would notice she was one of the only ladies not vying to display her musical talents.

Basically, she was escaping.

"I do hope you're not planning to hide here all night, my lady," Lord Maddox commented from the side.

Had he followed her? Unfortunately, the viscount stood on the side not blocked by the potted plant, so he had an unobstructed view of her nervous habit of crinkling her dress between her fingers.

She caught his gaze resting on her hands, so she smoothed her skirts and folded her hands in front of her, turning her attention back to the pianoforte. When Gemma's song came to an end, she stood and curtsied amidst a supply of enthusiastic applause, not the least of which was Lord Maddox's consort, Sir Wilde. His eyes fairly glowed with admiration of the lovely Gemma's musical gift.

"He seems well taken with her," Lord Maddox whispered near her. Far too near for propriety, Bridget thought.

She took a small step away from him and nodded her agreement, hoping he wouldn't notice the blush she felt staining her cheeks.

"Lady Gemma has many admirers."

She could feel the viscount's gaze burning into her and took another step to lengthen the distance between them.

His warmth seemed to draw nearer again, muddling her mind — distracting her from her surroundings. Why wouldn't he leave her alone? His breath rustled her hair as he leaned closer to whisper again. "Would you like to know whom I admire?"

Bridget shifted awkwardly. The room grew warmer by the moment. Then, as if Fate chose to intervene on her behalf, the next lady to entertain the group let loose a horrible screeching which tore through the room, causing both Bridget and the viscount to cringe in pain. It appeared to be enough to distract Lord Maddox from his train of thought, but the horrid sound issuing forth from the woman was an audible assault on sensitive ears.

"Is she dying?" Lord Maddox winced visibly as the voice reached towards the ceiling, taking the audience's ears as well as sanity with her.

"Likely," Bridget answered. "I don't think I've ever heard that particular note before."

"Perhaps we should throw something at her. In order to put her out of her misery."

"May I suggest pelting her with strawberries?" Bridget offered.

His pained smirk told her the comment hit its mark.

"They are the deadliest of the small fruits."

"You say that with such conviction, my lord." She covered her mouth with a gloved hand to suppress a giggle. At that moment, another wail reminiscent of a cow in labor assailed them. The collective gasp of the guests seemed to suck all the air from the room.

"Care to make an escape?" Lord Maddox asked with an innocent glint in his eyes. Bridget had no desire to be alone with him in any capacity, but she was in dire need of rescue. As it was, her ears threatened to bleed. If she remained where she was, she would surely go deaf. The idea of enduring more torture made her sick.

Another sour note vibrated the crystal chandelier, and Bridget made her hasty decision, placing her hand into her rescuer's grasp. "This doesn't mean I like you. Nor is this an invitation for you to practice the art of seduction." She felt the need to assure him of her disdain as he led her to the outdoor balcony.

"I wasn't under that assumption, my lady." Lord Maddox dropped her arm once they were outside. Unfortunately, she was mildly disappointed at the empty feeling it left her with. Was he truly only being polite to her now because it was expected? He was too unpredictable in his current state, and she found she couldn't read his emotions any better than she could decipher why her heart was nearly beating out of her chest when the man's eyes met hers from across the balcony.

"Is there a reason you are not on the list of entertainments this evening?" he asked. Bridget averted her gaze to the gardens beyond the balcony. "Oh, I see. You have no talent."

It wasn't a question, but rather a simple statement of fact. Even if he was correct in his assumption, it was hardly appropriate to throw a lady's shortcomings in her face. Her original assessment of his immeasurable arrogance was correct, and she could feel her aversion to him come seething back to the surface. It was good that he continued to insult her. Even better that his arrogance was so visible, then she could pretend she wasn't attracted to him in the least.

Bridget scowled. "I have more important aspirations than to entertain others who lack the ability to entertain themselves."

"Bravo!" Lord Maddox clapped his gloved hands together. "I couldn't agree more."

"W-with me?" Bridget stuttered. "You're agreeing with me?"

"Do you see anyone else out here with us?" Lord Maddox glanced about the balcony and shrugged. "It might be terribly forward to say this, but I believe a woman should have a good head on her shoulders. I despise those who think the only thing they have to flaunt is their beauty and ability with the pianoforte."

"You are the only man who feels that way, my lord."

"Many gentlemen feel as I do. They simply lack the courage to confess it aloud." He was moving toward her now, and she felt trapped as she tried in vain to inch away from him, finally finding herself backed up to a cold marble column. "You might find this hard to believe, but men are often afraid intelligent women will reject them."

"And yet they keep trying. Don't they, my lord?" He was too close. He was far too close. No matter what he said, Bridget promised herself she would not concede the field. Defense strategy. That is what she needed. And the best defense was often a good offense.

She offered him a sinfully sweet smile and waited for him to stop in his tracks. He didn't. Instead, he sauntered closer, slow but constant, until his face was inches from hers. Her breath quickened, and suddenly it seemed that air was in short supply even outside on the balcony.

"Yes, some of us don't understand the word *defeat*."

"Even when it comes in the form of strawberries?"

Bridget asked, fighting to control her breathing as the man drew nearer.

"Even when the lady threatens to push us in front of oncoming carriages and feed us the most grotesque fruit known to mankind. Even then, my lady. Even then." His smile dazzled her as he inclined his head and bestowed a soft lingering kiss on her lips.

The warm sensation of his tender kiss seeped into her bones. His lips were soft and hypnotic as they lightly moved across hers. A battle raged within her, and she couldn't decide if she should pull him closer or slap him across his perfect aristocratic face. So she waited, hoping the answer would come on its own.

She didn't have to wait long. As he withdrew, the victorious sparkle in his eye and the triumphant smirk spreading wide across his lips brought her the realization — he thought he'd won.

And then her hand flew on its own.

She only wished she had a handful of strawberries to add to the humiliation.

Chapter Five
Motivating Factors

"Bridget!" Aunt Latissia's voice split the silence, shattering the peaceful dream keeping Bridget abed. She groaned as the vision faded and rolled over to find her lady's maid laying out an afternoon dress.

A pounding on the door reminded her Aunt Latissia was still waiting on her response.

"I'm awake, Aunt!" she called. The door burst open, and the countess strode in dressed in her best receiving dress.

It was far too early for visitors. Let alone visitors worthy of such lengths taken to impress them. That left only one possible caller of consequence.

"Is Grandmother expected this morning?" The thought brought her abruptly from her somnolent haze, and she sat bolt upright.

"Yes, yes!" Aunt Latissia spat frantically. "Why are you still lounging about, girl? She'll be arriving any moment. Quickly! Tessa, help Lady Bridget with her dress and, for the love of Saint Peter, do something with that rat nest of hair!"

Of all the people in the world, the Dowager Countess of

Darlingshire had the most power to send Aunt Latissia reeling into a fit of the vapors. Bridget was not entirely unaffected in her presence either. In fact, the one pleasing aspect of her current arrangement to be sponsored by her aunt and uncle this season was that it got her out from under her grandmother's thumb.

Aunt Latissia spun through the room like a whirlwind then was gone as quickly as she came, leaving Bridget rushing to dress and ready herself. It would do no one any good to keep her grandmother waiting. The dowager was a tiny thing, and one wouldn't think it to look at her, but she had a frightful glower that could singe the flea off a dog at ten paces.

In nothing short than miraculous timing, Bridget was scurrying down the stairs to the sitting room as quickly as propriety would allow. She was well aware that her grandmother would expect nothing less, and she had no intention of letting the woman down.

Her stomach rumbled, but there was no time to break her fast this morning.

The maids were scurrying about the sitting room, while Aunt Latissia bellowed orders in a frenzy. The commotion was dizzying.

"Sit down, dear! Sit down!" her aunt said when she noticed Bridget enter the room. "Not there! The dowager will want that chair. Here... on the settee." The woman's eyes darted about the room in a fashion that spoke of madness.

Bridget couldn't help but feel some sympathy for the woman. They had, after all, been raised under the same stringent control. It was a wonder Aunt Latissia wasn't already relegated to the asylum! There were many times in that house Bridget would have preferred a room at Bedlam.

She took the seat indicated and straightened her skirts, hoping this would be a short visit. However, Bridget's grandmother rarely left her home to visit anyone, so the chances she was coming for a mere social call were quite slim.

Which meant…

Grandmother was coming on her account.

Which could only mean…

It would not be a pleasant morning.

Bridget drew in a deep, slow breath to soothe her nerves. It wouldn't do to lose her temper in her grandmother's presence. When she was growing up, any show of displeasure on Bridget's part was always referred to as a vulgar Irish tantrum.

Her grandmother hadn't cared for Bridget's Irish mother, noble blood or not, and she had made no secret of her disdain for that side of Bridget's lineage.

"Ahem." Francis's customary throat clearing sent a chill down Bridget's spine, which straightened and tensed as if on command. She folded her hands primly in her lap, crossed her ankles beneath her skirts, and looked to the doorway in utter apprehension.

"The Dowager Countess of Darlingshire," he announced in his proper monotone, not even a hint of the same dread that flowed through Bridget's veins at the very sound of the woman's name. But then, nothing ever upset Francis.

Aunt Latissia seemed frozen as well, but she stood along with Bridget to welcome the dowager.

"Good morning, Mother," Aunt Latissia gushed, the tremor in her voice was hardly noticeable as she curtsied in the most chaste fashion — she saved her scandalously low curtsies for the young gentlemen of the *ton*.

"Grandmother," Bridget said as she dipped in a brief curtsy.

"Let's dispense with the formalities, ladies. You know why I'm here," her grandmother said as she took her seat. Her voice was barely above a whisper. She never raised her voice. It would be improper. Her expressions were effective enough on their own.

"Yes, Mother." Aunt Latissia sat down, and Bridget

followed her lead.

The elderly woman trained her icy glare on Bridget.

"What is this I hear about you refusing to show favor to any gentleman?"

Bridget glanced at her aunt, whose gaze flitted up to the chandelier. Traitorous wench.

There was no escaping a direct question.

"I have found none to my liking, Grandmother."

The dowager clicked her tongue with contempt. "None to your liking, indeed. Let me be perfectly clear. You shall choose a gentleman. You shall acquire a proposal. And you shall be married by the end of the year... whether you like of it or not."

There was nothing left to be said.

To answer back would mean certain dire consequences that Bridget had no desire to endure. And how was she to explain to a woman like her grandmother her reasons for not wanting to marry? It was impossible for anyone to understand the world in which Bridget had grown up. The constant pressure, the rejection, and finally the betrayal, which had caused such scars that Bridget could think of nothing worse than being married to a man who had the power to break her heart.

The dowager scowled and grunted then turned her focus on Aunt Latissia, who squirmed under the weight of her mother's cold stare. "I entrusted you with this very simple task, Latissia. I am..." She closed her eyes momentarily for effect. "*Disappointed* in your incompetence. Bridget is a comely girl with a sizeable dowry. It should have been accomplished weeks ago. Your failure in this will not be tolerated. So if you have even a sliver of sense, you will set aside your own... *amorous* endeavors and attend to Bridget's."

Geneva entered in that moment with the tea service, interrupting the thick tension of the moment.

"I will not be staying for tea," the dowager said and rose from her seat. Aunt Latissia and Bridget rose with her. "You understand my instructions. See to it." She turned on her heel and was gone.

Bridget released the breath she had been holding and glanced at her aunt expecting a similar sigh of relief.

Instead the scowl on her aunt's face was reminiscent of an angry wolf deprived of her latest kill.

Slowly, Bridget lowered herself back into her seat and took up a cup of tea, avoiding eye contact for as long as possible, a strategy that soon proved to be ineffective.

Aunt Latissia stepped directly in front of her and glowered down at her, leveling an index finger in Bridget's face. "Now hear me. I shall *not*... endure *that* again. Tonight. At the ball. You shall affect a gentleman's attention. And I shall haunt your every move until you do so."

Chapter Six
Conceding the Bout

Self-consciously, Anthony raised his gloved hand to his cheek. The very same cheek on which Lady Bridget had indeed left a permanent impression the night previous. He saw it coming — saw the flash of anger in her eyes, the passion pulsing in her veins — as her breath grew labored, and finally the dainty gloved hand sailed through the air toward its target. He could have stopped it. After all, he had experienced such assaults from women who didn't appreciate his charms. Though in his life, it had happened exactly twice. Nevertheless, he still knew what to expect.

He smiled to himself as he strode toward the grand house. He wouldn't have moved for all the tea in China. It was necessary to give her the pleasure of the slap, for it meant she wouldn't have to feel guilty about taking pleasure in the kiss they shared, and he was entirely convinced she'd enjoyed it.

With a chuckle he reached his destination. The Duke of Hasbrough was throwing his annual ball, and Anthony knew Lady Bridget would be attending. Of course, all odds were against her speaking to him again after the stolen kiss. So he waited along the wall for that glorious red hair to appear amidst the bland storm of browns and yellows.

"There you are," he whispered to himself as he spied Lady Bridget entering the ballroom. Erring on the side of caution, he chose to take advantage of the element of surprise. Quite like a burglar, he snuck up behind her, reached for her arm, and managed to sweep her onto the dance floor before her aunt realized she was gone.

"I don't believe you're on my card, my lord," Lady Bridget said through her teeth. Another advantage — she wouldn't make a scene. She didn't want the attention.

"I'm claiming this dance, and all the rest of them, unless you give me a minute of your time. I have a proposition for you."

His words were met with an exaggerated eye roll. "Do you really wish to proposition me, at the ball? Truly? Do you wish to be turned down in front of everyone, or perhaps even slapped?"

With great strength Anthony refrained from laughing aloud. "It seems to me that your definition of proposition and mine are clearly different. You make it sound as though I'm trying to get you into my bed."

Lady Bridget flushed. "Well, I—"

"And dare I say your cheeks have turned a rosy pink?" Anthony set her to a twirl and pulled her indecently close.

"I wasn't referring to your lewd lifestyle, my lord, and I am not blushing! I—" Lady Bridget's chest rose and fell rapidly in either irritation or passion; he wasn't certain which — not that there was a terrible difference between the two where this woman was concerned.

"Sadly, my proposition has nothing to do with mistresses or beds, though I wouldn't be entirely opposed to the idea if you were intent on offering yourself like a lamb to the slaughter."

Lady Bridget's eyes widened. She opened her mouth to

speak, but Anthony interrupted her.

"It has been said one night in my bed is better than hundreds with other men. Surely you know my reputation is to first seek to please the woman. To caress her body with my eyes, using my hands in so many ways as to heighten her passion..." He lifted his gloved hand and briefly touched her neck. "But sadly, as you say, you are not propositioning me, I was propositioning you — and for something entirely boring, I assure you."

Lady Bridget's eyes darted around, taking in everything and everyone but him. Clearly, she was uncomfortable, and he silently cursed himself for coming on so strong.

"I need your help." He said *help* very quietly, for he despised the vile word.

"Kelp?" Lady Bridget glanced at him. "Is your stomach ailing you, my lord?"

"Devil take it, I said *help*!" He all but yelled, inviting stares from several women nearby who appeared more than inclined to offer aid.

"What could the great Viscount Maddox possibly need with my help?"

He hated how beautiful his name sounded on her lips — despised that his blood was near boiling with desire for her. And the feel of her body beneath his gloves was the most pleasurable of pain. The dance was drawing to an end, but he needed more time.

"Trust me. I mean to talk with you about this, but the dance is ending."

She tried to protest, which just made him hold her hand all the tighter. He led her down the hall to the first room on the left, first checking for any sort of company and then closing the doors silently behind them.

"If you come near to touch me, my lord. I swear to you, I'll scream." Lady Bridget was standing behind the nearest chair, apparently needing a barrier between them.

"If I touch you without your consent, I promise you that you may scream and impale me with my own knife." He slipped it out of his boot and slid it across the floor to her.

She picked it up and clenched it in her hand. Her eyebrow lifted in suspicion. "Well? What is so urgent that you feel the need to drag me into a private room against my will?"

Anthony took a deep breath. He had already decided to tell her all. "I never lose bets."

"Is that why you've brought me here? To tell me you never lose? Truly, my lord, your arrogance is astounding."

"Hear me out." He grew flustered as Bridget tilted her head and put her hands on her hips. The same hips he held just moments ago. He turned around, needing to gain his wits lest he find himself impaled on the business end of his own knife. "My brother and Wilde have issued me a challenge." She didn't change her expression, but her impatience was evident in the tapping of her fingers on her hips. "They have given me four weeks to win a certain woman's affection. Four weeks, or I will lose."

Lady Bridget laughed. "Four weeks? To woo a woman? I was right, only a man with an ungodly amount of pride would take such a challenge."

"If it was any other woman I would have already been crowned victorious." Anthony fired back. "It just so happens they have chosen the most obstinate woman in the *ton*."

"My lord, I have no experience in wooing women. What makes you think I would be of any assistance? Do you wish for me to help you make her jealous? If that is what you need, surely any number of the debutantes in the other room would be more likely candidates." Her gaze traveled around the room as if in boredom. "I suppose it's only natural you would choose a woman with no interest in you for the task."

"That's not exactly what I had in mind, my lady." She was scrutinizing the floral pattern on the upholstered chair before her. "In fact, I have already determined I will undoubtedly lose this challenge." Her gaze returned to his face almost in triumph over his failure.

"If that is the case, why have this conversation? Why try to enlist my aid?" Her victorious smirk drove home the realization that this was truly his only option left.

"Lady Bridget," he answered with a heavy sigh. "*You* are the object of my challenge." A hint of surprise flashed briefly in her clear blue eyes, and her expression softened. "I concede the bet. Your disdain for me is insurmountable." Lady Bridget appeared as though she would speak, but Anthony cut her off quickly with a wave of his hand. "I know how you abhor my ego, but I do wish to save some dignity if possible. If it helps at all, my brother's arrogance is far more intolerable than my own. To lose to him would ensure a lifetime of humiliation. And while I am certain, given your inclination toward pleasure at my demise, you would thoroughly enjoy the entertainments, my own fragile confidence would be unable to withstand the torture. I would die an unhappy, alone, and bitter bachelor in the country. Do you truly want that on your conscience, my lady?"

The silence hung heavy at the end of his proposition. The lady's expression was unreadable. Anthony had naught to do but wait for her to present her terms.

"Answer me this, for I'm terribly curious. When would you have won my favor, do you think, my lord? Would it have been the day you assumed I was blind?" She toyed with the knife in her hands and stepped around the chair, moving closer to him. "Or perhaps after you slipped on an innocent strawberry?" She was drawing nearer, and with every step Anthony grew warmer. "Or maybe after you fell on the street? Would it have been then, my lord?" She stopped directly in front of him and grinned the wide grin of the victor.

"Those were flukes." Anthony cursed. "They haven't happened before, I assure you! It's all your fault anyway, you have me…"

"I have you what?" Lady Bridget breathed the air directly in front of him. He couldn't inhale without her scent invading his senses.

"You have me… somewhat flustered."

"I'm sure that was very hard to admit." Her eyes twinkled with amusement.

"Yes, well, just so you're aware, I have half a mind to ravish you right here just to prove to myself that I still can."

Lady Bridget's eyes widened for a second, then she turned her face away from him. "So my choice is to leave you to your own devices, or offer my aid, is that it?"

Anthony swore. What the devil was he doing? What was she doing to him? "If you help me convince my brother and Wilde that you are, in fact, smitten with me, I'll convince your aunt that we're courting, thereby making it possible for you to escape this Season free of the pressures from your family."

He knew he had her by the irritated look on her face. A look he recognized as the one women only wore when they realized a man was right. She was caught — gloriously caught — for he had found her Achilles' heel, and he meant to use it to his fullest advantage, in whatever way possible.

"Think of it this way…" He began to pace, slowly circling her, deep in thought. He stopped when he stood behind her and moved to gently rest his hands on her shoulders. "If you fall in love with me, and I cry off at the end of the Season, your aunt will be more than understanding in your need to nurse your broken heart. And I am a difficult man to get over… Why, it may take you months — perhaps even years."

A laugh escaped Lady Bridget's throat, though she tried to stifle it with her hand. "Yes, and my poor soul would be so fearful of seeing the great Viscount Maddox at the Season's events, I would surely take to my bed with a broken heart."

"It would be expected," Anthony agreed, his hands sliding down her arms.

"After all, you are highly sought after."

"Many a tender-hearted girl would be sick with melancholy…"

She set her shoulders with apparent resolve, and he knew she had made a decision. Slowly, he turned her to face him. Her scent again invaded his senses, causing his body to tense with want. He would do well to remember she wasn't his to possess. He knew she was weakening, that she saw the obvious advantage to his plan, but he wished to hear her say it aloud.

"What do you say?" His eyes locked with hers.

"I agree, but you must promise to keep your hands off me, my lord. It cannot be said that you ruined me, do you understand?" She brushed his hands off her arms without emotion.

"Perfectly," he swore, allowing his arms to fall to his sides in surrender.

Rolling her eyes, a smile broke out on her face. "It's kind of you to so readily agree, but I am serious. No kissing, no caressing, no—"

Anthony clapped his hand over her mouth. If she continued to speak thus she would find herself good and ruined. "Fine." He thought his heart might explode. "I will agree to your terms, only please don't say anything else. Such words do not help my current state of interest with your body, my lady." He swallowed the knot in his throat. Then allowed mischief to play in his expression. "Shall we seal it with a kiss?"

She glared. The cold steel of the knife blade rested at his chest, serving as a subtle reminder.

"So, is that a no?"

The room shifted. It seemed the lady suddenly realized what a compromising position she was in. The air in the room grew heavy, as did her eyes, and her gaze shot to the knife in her hand; her long eyelashes fluttered down to rest across her cheekbones in embarrassment. But not before an ever-so-brief moment of focus spent on his lips.

Not truly fearing the blade she held to him, he reached for her head and coaxed it toward his, planting a passionate kiss on her lips.

The knife dropped to the floor.

Anthony wrapped his hands around her waist, lifting her in the air to pull her closer still.

The haze descended upon his mind in a dense fog of desire. The promise he had just made seemed only a dream, quickly dissolving in the heat of his need for her.

A sharp pain in his shin brought him hurdling back into clarity. Had she just kicked him? As if in answer to his unspoken question, a torrent of pointed blows rained on his legs — all proudly distributed by the woman he was now assaulting.

With a curse he dropped her; she sailed to the floor.

"Don't ever do that again," she said, breathless upon the floor at his feet. A glance at her was enough to ruin him even now, for her chest heaved with rapid gasps and the fire in her eyes matched the particular glint of her hair.

After a moment, Anthony found his voice again. "I am sorry." He cursed again. "Don't worry. I will keep my end of the bargain. However, I must add that tasting you is worth the torture you inflict. I give you my word to maintain a respectable distance, though few things are better than tasting of the forbidden fruit."

"And I am the forbidden fruit?" Lady Bridget asked as she stood and straightened her skirts.

"It might be best if I think of you as a strawberry." He winked. "Then it will become infinitely easier to maintain my distance."

She laughed lightly. "Perhaps so."

"Shall we return to the ball then? We have people to convince that you're utterly besotted with me."

"Don't forget." Lady Bridget reached for the knife and

handed it to him. "They must also believe you're besotted with me."

Anthony took the knife and shook his head as he slid it back into his boot. "My dear, that will require no acting whatsoever on my part." He held out his arm. Tentatively, she took it and they returned to the ballroom.

In Anthony's mind, a hush descended when everyone saw the girl secured to his arm. If she thought him prideful before, she would shudder to see how much his chest was puffed now. He brought her gloved hand to his lips and kissed it, tightly pulling her along back onto the dance floor.

"Ah, so the rumors begin," Anthony whispered near her ear. "Do you think you can manage?"

They separated as the dance demanded. When they drew back together, Lady Bridget winked. "I shall just have to endure you, won't I?"

"Endure is such a terrible sounding word. I much prefer *enjoy, take advantage of, seduce...*" He trailed off, noting her heightened color.

"Endure," she repeated. "Definitely endure. I believe I'll deserve a medal for having to deal with the sheer magnitude of your lordship's ego for the remaining weeks."

"And I shall be only too happy to secure it around your beautiful neck." Anthony battled against his desire to touch her flushed skin once more. This was not going to be easy.

She didn't answer him, merely raised her brow and curtsied as the dance ended, and it was just in time, for Wilde approached and asked a dance of the girl.

Anthony conceded, mainly because a man who didn't know how to properly seduce a woman was not a threat. He watched as Wilde awkwardly took her hand, as if he was nervous. Anthony shook the thought from his head and approached his smug twin.

"I believe I've won," Anthony announced.

"You cheated." Ambrose cursed.

"I never cheat."

"Says the cheater."

"Speaking of cheating — have you seen your wife? She's promised to show me how to best you at chess later this week."

Ambrose cleared his throat. "Yes, well, she's only won a handful of times. That doesn't mean she's better at anything..."

"Right." Anthony patted his brother on the back, then reached for a flute of champagne as it passed. "So, her whereabouts?"

"Spying."

Anthony spewed the contents of his mouth into the air, missing his brother by a mere inch. "So, she does your dirty work for you? I see how it is."

Ambrose glared. "Merely trying to acquire more information for your benefit, brother, and she so graciously offered to help."

"Probably wants to see me married off so I stop bothering you two." Anthony picked up another flute of champagne.

He lifted it to his lips as Ambrose swore. "It's just that you come at the most inappropriate times, just yesterday we barely had time to clothe—"

Anthony spewed the champagne again, this time spraying his brother well in the face. "Devil take it, Ambrose! I need not know the details! Besides," he glanced over at the sound of Lady Bridget's laughter in Wilde's arms. "She's as good as mine."

"That confident, eh, Anthony?" Ambrose brooded, wiping the dripping champagne from his face with his handkerchief.

"Yes." He downed the contents of his glass. "Yes, I am."

Chapter Seven
So Goes the Battle

It would accomplish two tasks at once. And Bridget was nothing if not efficient. Yes, she agreed to help the viscount. But not for his sake.

Her benefits would far outweigh the drawbacks of spending time in the company of his acute arrogance. Her aunt and uncle would no longer find need to scrutinize her every move at a social event. More importantly, the viscount had vowed to keep his advances to himself. Bridget was assured she had nothing to fear from constant assaults on her resolve to keep her virtue intact. And heaven help her, it was disintegrating in leaps and bounds every time he touched her.

After the dance with Sir Wilde, Bridget made her way back to where her aunt sat in predatory anticipation of her next quarry. The woman's gaze scoured the gentlemen, seeking out the weakest of the herd. It made Bridget's stomach turn. And she was at a loss at how her aunt's blatant disregard for propriety could go so unnoticed amongst the *ton*. And then there was poor Uncle Ernest, who was a kind but preoccupied man, completely oblivious to his wife's indiscretions.

As she grew closer, Aunt Latissia regarded her with suspicion. "You're very cozy with Viscount Maddox this evening." Her rapacious glance back at Lord Maddox was hardly veiled. "Are you certain you wish to have your name linked with such as he?"

"Are you displeased, my lady? I was under the impression you believed him a worthy suitor. After all, you often seek his company, do you not?" Bridget said with a hint of irony. Aunt Latissia's sharp look told her the point was not lost on her, but in that moment Uncle Ernest approached, cutting off the vicious scolding sure to come.

"Bridget. My lady," he addressed them, kissing his wife's proffered hand. "How do you find the dancing this evening?"

"It's lovely, Uncle," Bridget answered.

"I do believe our young charge has finally found someone worthy of her attention, my lord," Latissia said with concealed bitterness.

"That's wonderful, my dear! Who is our lucky young gentleman?" Uncle Ernest was fairly bursting with pleasure at the news.

Bridget knew that neither of her guardians was so concerned with her happiness as they were with regaining their freedom from the responsibility bestowed upon them in her behalf.

"Lord Maddox," her aunt answered. "But I don't know if that is a match I can approve—"

"Nonsense!" the earl interrupted. "It is an excellent match, and we shall do our part to encourage this courtship, my dear! You know his reputation and influence. We could do no better short of the royal family!"

"Of course, my lord. I thought only of our sweet niece's delicate sensitivities when it comes to living under the scrutiny of the *ton*. And the viscount has a way of drawing attention as you know..."

Bridget knew her aunt's objections had more to do with

her futile hopes to seduce the viscount for herself and far less to do with any sense of what Bridget's desires might be.

Her uncle shook his head resolutely. "This is an excellent match. And we will encourage it." With that, he kissed his wife's hand once again, bowed briefly to Bridget, and made his way to the gentleman's lounge.

As he left them, Lady Burnside concealed her wrath under a thin veil of pleasantries. Through clenched teeth, she said, "Very well. Lord Maddox it is. Be sure to smile, my dear. Your usual glower will do nothing to entice his lordship to seek your hand."

"Aunt, I don't think—"

"Precisely. You don't think. Now, you heard your uncle. We will encourage it. It is your job to secure a husband, my dear. Do not let your grandmother down."

"Yes, Aunt."

Lady Burnside stood quiet for a moment as if deep in thought before adding, "He will have to see your talents..." She considered another moment then waved an over-eager hand at Lord Maddox, who eyed them from across the room.

At her aunt's invitation, he sauntered toward them with that air of self-assurance that bothered Bridget all the way to her toes.

"Lord Maddox," Lady Burnside crooned upon his arrival near their party. "We are simply dying to have you visit tomorrow afternoon. Lady Bridget has a painting lesson, and is in dire need of a subject." She jostled Bridget with a sharp elbow.

Lord Maddox's gaze turned on her with an eyebrow raised in curiosity. "Is that so?" he asked.

"Yes, my lord," Bridget said with a sigh. "Will you consent to a portrait, sir?" Suddenly, her side of their bargain did not seem to be going the way she had hoped. If this interference by her aunt was any indication of what she could expect, she would not see any benefit from this arrangement whatsoever.

****

Oh, heaven was surely smiling upon him! Sit for a portrait? Spend hours in her company doing nothing save staring at her delicate hand as it sashayed this way and that? He cleared his throat. Above all he couldn't seem too eager to simply sit and stare. What would people think of him? Blast, he was already judging himself.

A servant passed by with champagne. Anthony quickly lifted a flute and drank the dry contents. "Yes, I believe that would be exciting indeed. Anything I can do to aid the lovely Lady Bridget in her... artistic pursuits." With his free hand he reached for her arm and looped it within his. "After all, I can think of nothing I would rather do than gaze upon your beauty, my sweet." He bit his lip.

Lady Burnside cleared her throat. "Lovely. We shall expect you in the afternoon. Shall we say around two?"

"Perfect. I wouldn't miss it for the world." Anthony winked at Lady Bridget and turned back toward her aunt, who was now changing to such a peculiar shade of red, he was sure her head would explode. Clearly, the woman was not amused that he had found a younger more desirable girl upon whom to shower his affections. He quickly excused himself and decided to call it a night. After all, he had much work to do the following afternoon.

****

Anthony gazed upon the large regal mansion and steeled himself for what would surely be the one of the more trying experiences of his life. Sitting for hours in the presence of the most attractive woman in the world as she painted didn't seem to be the best of ideas, especially if his current state of arousal was any indication of how the day would proceed.

The idea that he would be required to stand utterly still while having to stare at the beautiful Lady Bridget was near laughable. After all, simply being in her presence accelerated his breathing, his desire, his irritation — everything.

He must remember his part of the bargain. No matter how much she seemed to need it, Anthony had promised to keep his hands to himself. Now if he could just keep his own desires in check, lest he embarrass himself and the girl in the process.

Anthony knocked on the door and was quickly ushered into one of the salons. Bridget stood behind a large easel, paintbrush in hand.

"Am I late?" he asked, his voice cracking the silence of the room.

"Just on time." She didn't look at him. Instead her dainty hand added a few more strokes to the painting before her. The lady tilted her head and a smile broke across her face.

"What are you working on?" He couldn't help the playful smile that spread across his lips.

"A masterpiece." She huffed and threw him a saucy wink.

"May I see it?" He felt his smile widening.

Bridget pulled away from the painting and shrugged. "Of course, my lord. I do hope it doesn't scare you though. It may be frightening."

"Frightening?" He gave her a patronizing look and turned to face the picture.

"A bowl of strawberries?" he asked, like the idiot he was.

Lady Bridget sighed. "Yes, I felt inspired."

"Obviously."

"And did you notice that in the corner?" She pointed to the top of the piece where, what had to be the ugliest man alive stood, arms high above his head flailing as if he was about to take a tumble.

"It's you!" She laughed. "It's quite a likeness, don't you agree?"

Anthony gave a tight smile. "Yes, it's perfect. Though you forgot one detail."

"What?"

"The woman standing next to me who threw the strawberry, perpetuating the entire tragic sequence of events."

"I did nothing of the sort!"

Anthony snorted. "So you say, my lady, but I have seen your true colors. You'd be much happier impaling me on the end of your paintbrush than standing next to me right now. Admit it."

"With pride."

Anthony muttered a low string of curses and eyed her with suspicion. "Where is your aunt this afternoon?"

"Gone."

"Gone?" His voice raised a few octaves.

Lady Bridget smiled. "Lady Burnside is rarely home in the afternoons, my lord. She is making calls. I don't expect her home for several hours."

"You," he pointed at Lady Bridget and tried not to yell, "are not allowed to speak of any of this to anyone, do you understand? After all, I do have my reputation to consider."

"Perfectly."

"Good—"

"Not only," she interrupted, "do I have to endure your presence for the next two weeks but I'm not allowed to speak of it to any human being save the one man I would rather spit on than talk to."

"Lies."

"What?" She set down her paintbrush and crossed her arms.

"I didn't misspeak. I said *lies*. All of it. You like me."

"You arrogant man!" Lady Bridget poked him in the chest. "I want nothing to do with you. I want—"

"Me. You want me. There's no use denying it. But never fear. I'll be patient for you to come to your senses." He began stripping his coat and gloves.

"W-what are you doing, my lord?"

"Anthony. It's Anthony, and I shall call you Bridget, or perhaps my stubborn little temptress. They are one and the same, I assure you."

"Anthony," she ground out through clenched teeth. "Would you please explain why you are removing your outer garments?"

"You mean, why am I getting naked?"

Bridget flushed and covered her eyes. A soft gasp escaped the throat of the maid sitting in the corner. "My lord, really—"

"Ah, you have to use my name."

"Anthony," she squeaked, still shielding her eyes. "Why are you taking off your clothes?"

He shrugged. "I thought you meant to paint me?"

"I did. I-I do." She took another steadying breath and turned away from him. "But I'd much prefer to do so while you are fully clothed, if you don't mind."

"Pity." He shook his head and smiled at her back. He was just trying to unsettle her, but when he noticed her peeking through her fingers, his masculine pride swelled markedly. Perhaps he would have gone through with it. Yes, she would be ruined. She would be all his, and he would have her — whether she wanted to be had or not.

"Shall we begin?" She still hadn't turned back to face him. Most likely her face was scarlet with embarrassment.

"I'm ready when you are." His voice was low, seductive, and coaxing.

Bridget shook her head, and an unruly strand of red silken hair fell out of her coiffure. She returned to the easel and set a new blank canvas on it. "Now, we both know you're here merely to vex me and taunt my aunt. By all appearances, it will look like we're courting, so you only need to stay for an hour or so."

"And if I want to stay forever?" he asked taking a seat on the settee.

"Anthony—" She put her hands on her hips. "I choose to ignore your asinine insinuation. Please remember our bargain. Now, sit still so I can paint you."

"With my clothes on," he half-grumbled.

The canvas blocked her face, but he could have sworn he heard her giggle. "Yes, with your clothes on. And if you start disrobing again, I'm going to paint you with strawberries."

"I understand." His voice was laced with irritation. "By all means, paint my demise. Death by strawberry. It seems to be the theme of my life."

Bridget sighed behind the canvas. "Fine. What would you like sitting next to you?"

Anthony chuckled. She shouldn't have asked such a question. Her virgin ears were going to burn by the time he was finished with her. He cleared his throat.

"I desire to be lying across the settee, much like this." He demonstrated. Bridget peeked around the canvas.

"Brilliant."

"I'm not done."

She sighed. "Naturally."

"I should also like to be painted with a lady next to me."

Bridget paused. "And this lady, dare I ask — what shall she be doing?"

Anthony laughed. "What all ladies do when in a compromising position. I'd like her to be kissing my neck, just here." He pointed to his neck.

Bridget didn't look.

"Bridget? You aren't looking. How are you to know how to paint if you do not look?"

"I c-can imagine," she stammered.

"No. I have seen your work when you aren't looking at a

model. And as a paying customer—" He paused to lay a farthing on the table. "I demand you look and give me what I ask for."

Slowly, the girl peeked around the canvas, her face a brilliant shade of red.

"Right here." Anthony pointed again. "And I should like her hair to be red. A vibrant red — wild like she is. Her eyes must be blue, for I find blue eyes to be the most entrancing. And her smile... truly, you don't want to get me started on her smile."

Her breathing became laborious as he looked at her and grinned. "The way this lady smiles is like the sunrise. I should like you to paint that for me, though I know it will be difficult... to paint perfection."

"You're a horrible flirt, Anthony."

Anthony closed his eyes and let out a sigh. "I'm no more a horrible flirt than you are a horrible tease."

"A tease?" She threw her paintbrush onto her palette and marched over to him. "How dare you say that, how dare you—"

"Ah, You are so very fetching when you are vexed, my lady." He motioned for her to take a seat next to him.

Rolling her eyes, she let out an irritated huff before sitting down. "A tease?" she repeated.

"Making you angry is the only way I have discovered that will coax to come near me. Truly, I am desperate enough to try anything to force you to speak to me. Now, let us talk of the upcoming ball."

"What about it?" Lady Bridget's eyes darted to the ground, obviously irritated.

"Well." Anthony scooted away to give her space. "We will need to seem more familiar to those around us. I, for one, shall call you sweeting, as well as Bridget." Her name tasted like honey on his tongue. He had to clear his throat to mask the desire he felt in that moment. "And you should call me

Adonis."

"Surely we do not need pet names for one another—"

"Yes," he interrupted. "I believe we do. And you cannot appear so irritated around me either. Nobody will believe you're infatuated, especially my brother. Your aunt is quite another story. She's going to be looking for any excuse to separate us."

"I may let her." Bridget sighed.

Anthony glared. "If you let her near me I'll, I'll—" Blast. Why couldn't he think of a good enough threat?

"Stutter?" Bridget tilted her head and offered him a malicious smirk.

He cursed and shook his head. "I'll simply attach myself to your person, like a leech, and we both know how much you enjoy my company."

"Ah, finally comparing yourself to a similar species. Good for you." She patted his knee then pulled back her hand as if burned. "I, um… I should get back to painting you. I mean, that is to say, I should be finishing your portrait, so if you could manage not to say anything offensive in the next hour or so, I'll proceed."

"By all means." Anthony motioned to the easel. "I'll try not to interrupt. Though it might be difficult. I can be quite distracting."

"I am certain I can withstand your many charms, my lord."

"Anthony," he corrected.

"Anthony." She blushed and returned to the easel. But not before Anthony took great pleasure in watching her hips sway as she walked back to her place.

****

Bridget knew she had to spend some time with him in order to hold up her end of the bargain, but his presence in her life was more of an inconvenience. It was nice to have a live model to paint for once, but if live was the only requirement, perhaps a rabid polecat would be preferable.

Not that Lord Maddox... er, *Anthony,* was entirely unpleasant to look at. In fact, he had a rather unsettling effect on her whenever he was near. His soft brown hair and golden emerald eyes drew her gaze like a moth to flame. She told herself it was only as an artist appreciating beauty. Nothing more than that.

Honestly, if it wasn't for his unbearable arrogance and vain utterings, she might quite enjoy the view. *Adonis* was a description not far off the mark.

Bridget sighed and shook her head to clear the fog. The portrait. She was supposed to be painting.

He was right. He was nothing if not distracting. And Bridget didn't care for distractions. Not when there were so many other noble pursuits to occupy her attention.

Drat! Her novel! She had almost forgotten about it! How was that even possible?

One word. Anthony.

There was very little recourse for revenge in situations like these. And his familiarity today was well deserving of some sort of comeuppance. Bridget glanced around the room in scheming defiance until her gaze came to rest on the bowl of strawberries sitting on the table behind him.

A slow, deliberate smirk creased her lips, and she set back to work on the portrait with renewed vigor.

"What are you plotting?" Anthony crooned from his place on the settee.

"Never you mind. Just sit still and try not to spoil my masterpiece."

When she finished, she covered the canvas with a thick cloth, veiling it from Anthony's view.

"Aren't you going to let me see it?" He took a step around her and made an effort to lift the cloth.

"Don't touch!" Bridget slapped at his hand, but he dodged out of her reach.

"Hours of silent torture, and you won't even let me have a peek?"

"No. I want to put the finishing touches on it. You will have to wait, *Adonis*."

A wicked smile spread over his face as he glanced at her with an unholy gleam in his eyes. "See how naturally it rolls off the tongue? I believe we might be able to pull this off after all, dear Bridget." He stepped toward her and brushed the stray tendril of hair from her face, catching her hand in his.

Bridget's breath caught in her throat as he lifted her hand to his lips, holding it there much longer than proper. His gaze held hers.

When the maid cleared her throat, Bridget jolted and pulled her hand abruptly away from Anthony's grasp.

"I forgot she was in here," he whispered with a disappointed smirk.

"I believe it's time for you to take your leave, my lord," Bridget announced. She kept her voice steady though his nearness had caused her to tremble.

"Very well, my dear. I shall look forward to the unveiling of the portrait the next time I call. Good evening, *sweeting*," he said with a wink, then spun on his heel and let himself out.

Chapter Eight
Beyond the Call of Duty

"Are you sure we should doing this?" Gemma whispered as Bridget stepped through the bookseller's door. The girl could be dreadfully taxing.

"Of course, sweet Gemma," she coaxed as she tugged at her friend's arm. "I have been here many times with my uncle. It is quite proper, I assure you." Lying should not come as easily as it did, but she needed Gemma's help if she was to pull this off. After all, if she was to write a novel worthy of reading, she must read what was popular, even if it was scandalous for a woman to do so.

The doubt was apparent in Gemma's sapphire eyes when they pushed open the door, but she allowed herself to be pulled into the dimly lit shop.

Bridget knew exactly what book she wanted, but it was in the gentleman's section. A distraction was in order. She turned to her maid, who had followed behind them.

"Tessa, won't you wait outside the door to direct his lordship when he comes?" The maid stared at her blankly for a moment, no doubt thinking she had gone quite mad.

Of course, it was a lie. No man was coming behind them, but the ruse might work to keep the clerk from chasing her back to the ladies' stacks. She began there, naturally, not wanting to draw attention too soon. Browsing through the mindless romance novels on the shelves was the perfect pretense.

Beside her, Gemma relaxed visibly. Poor, sweet Gemma. She had likely never set foot inside a bookseller's shop, let alone read through anything more stimulating than the works of Mrs. Burney.

Bridget glanced at the clerk behind her. He was scrutinizing them sharply over his spectacles, as if expecting at any moment they would lunge for the gentlemen's shelves. Small talk would be just the thing to desensitize the bookseller to the female presence.

"Gemma, it seems as though I haven't seen you in an age. What have you been doing with yourself lately?" Bridget began, hoping to lull the man into a false sense of security.

"I have received a number of afternoon calls of late." Gemma's voice was noticeably quieter than Bridget's had been. Her eyes darted nervously around the room.

"Oh? Any gentlemen I know?" The tone in her friend's voice drew Bridget's undivided attention, and she noticed Gemma fidgeting with the cuff of her glove. A mannerism she recognized as one of her dear friend's tells. Did she hold a secret tender for a young man? How had Bridget missed this?

"One in particular." Gemma's face colored with slight embarrassment.

Bridget was not one to enjoy such conversation usually, but her companion appeared to be concealing some news and perhaps desired Bridget to pry it out of her.

"Well, come then, Gemma. Don't keep me in such suspense. Who is the gentleman?" she prodded, taking a step in the general direction of the men's books.

"I'm not sure it's proper to speak of such things in

public," Gemma whispered again, her voice hardly more than a breath as she followed Bridget's lead.

Gemma had never behaved so tight-lipped before when it came to speaking of gentlemen. Her goal of marriage was no secret to Bridget. It made no sense now that Gemma would be suddenly shy to discuss such things. No one else was in the shop besides the two of them and the clerk.

"If you would rather discuss something else, we can return to this subject at a more proper time," Bridget reassured her, returning her attention to the task at hand. From her vantage point at the edge of the ladies' shelves, she could see her true objective. A fresh copy of Mary Wollstonecraft's *Vindication* was on the table directly behind the clerk.

"Do any of these strike your fancy, Gemma?"

Gemma's eyes grew wide, and she shook her head. "Bridget, I don't think we should be buying books in public," she whimpered.

"Oh, Gemma! You are a precious thing!" Bridget laughed. "Where else should one buy books?" Gemma had been raised to be so uptight and proper it was a wonder she was able to walk around in public at all without swooning.

"I don't know. It just seems so... so... scandalous." Her wide blue eyes darted around the room in obvious concern.

"Nonsense, Gemma! I told you, my uncle has brought me here many times."

"But, Bridget," she murmured. "Your uncle is a man."

Could Gemma really be so fearful of impropriety?

"Ahem." The clerk had sidled up beside them. "Are you ladies in need of assistance today?" The very tone in which he patronized them made Bridget's skin crawl. Seeds of indignation took root in her chest.

"I believe we've made our selections, sir." Bridget grabbed two novels from the shelf and stepped around the man to the counter, slipping Wollstonecraft's book beneath her other acquisitions with a stealthy hand.

He followed close behind, meeting her at the counter. "Will there be anything else, miss?"

"These will be all for today," Bridget said with what she believed was her most confident smile. She hoped her tremulous hands wouldn't betray her anxiety. He began to write a receipt for her purchases, as she worked to distract him from the titles by making small talk.

"It has been lovely weather of late, has it not?"

"Yes, lovely," he answered, not lifting his gaze from his task. He made quick work of writing up the first two titles — mindless romance novels written for women. Bridget tried to break his concentration once more.

"I dare say—" she began, but he cut her off.

"My lady." He lifted the coveted book and leveled his gaze at her. "I believe you have picked this up by mistake." The clerk scrutinized her down his long pointed nose over the wire rim of his spectacles. Gemma squirmed beside her.

"I'm certain I picked it up on purpose, sir," Bridget said. She had mastered a deadpan expression, which she used in situations just like this. If she appeared unflustered, it was usually the clerk who backed down first. So while her insides fluttered and twisted into knots, her outward countenance betrayed nothing of the inner turmoil. "I wish to purchase these three volumes."

But he did not back down. If anything, he grew more combative.

"This particular book is not suitable for young ladies of genteel breeding."

Lovely. He was one of *those*.

Bridget drew in a slow deliberate breath, shoring up her ire for the battle. The little pompous fool. He had no idea whom he was dealing with. But he would soon. And he would surely regret challenging her Irish temper with his repulsive male condescension.

"Listen to me, you wretched uncouth little man—" She

lifted a finger to point in his face with not a care for proper etiquette. Gemma shrieked in sheer horror, taking a step backward. But it was too late. Bridget could feel the fury engulfing her.

****

From a block away, Anthony recognized Bridget's maid standing alone outside the bookseller's shop. Perhaps he could pretend to be strolling by and happen upon her. The gossip would spread that he was out shopping with her, and by tonight his brother would be choking on his loss.

Smiling, he quickly crossed the street and tipped his hat to the maid. As his hand reached for the door he stole a glance through the shop window.

And was just in time to see two tiny fists pump into the air and reach out for the clerk's collar.

Anthony swore under his breath, jerked open the door, and marched over to where Bridget was on the verge of assaulting the man. The clerk covered his face with a book while she was making quick work of lunging across the counter, both hands still reaching for his shirt as if choking him would cause the problem to dissipate.

"Ah, just in time! Thank you so very much, sweeting, for grabbing these books for me. I lost track of the hour. Apologies. Will you ever forgive me?" Anthony uttered the entire speech in such a fluid voice he shocked even himself.

Bridget turned her cold stare on him mid-strangle, and for a moment he wanted to run back out the door.

"Y-y-you are quite mad, my lady!" The clerk's face was red with fury, and his eyes wide with fright. "Do you know this lady, my lord?"

Anthony chose that moment to pull the book from the clerk's still trembling hands. "Why of course, she's my betrothed. Isn't that right, my dear?"

Bridget still wasn't talking, but in her defense it seemed to be the wiser course of action since the expression on her face was evidence enough that she had not yet returned to a proper state of mind.

"And I was so eager to get my hands on a copy of…" Anthony stole a glance at the book and cursed aloud.

Bridget's mouth curved upwards into a tiny smile. The minx!

Anthony cleared his throat. "A copy of *A Vindication of the Rights of Woman*." It was quite surprising that he didn't choke over that mouthful. Not that he had anything against women's rights; he just wasn't the sort to go advertising his beliefs by buying such books.

Shaking his head, he pulled out the second book, and thankful it was a gothic tale, he reached into his pocket to produce some notes for the poor man whom his redhead had come nigh unto beating within an inch of his trebly worthless life.

The clerk shook his head and barked an indignant laugh. "Well, that explains it. I couldn't imagine such a proper young thing reading such a big book. It does nothing but fill her head with ideas, and we wouldn't want…"

Anthony froze and slowly lifted his head to give the clerk his most intimidating stare, stopping the man mid-sentence. "No, please, finish what you were going to say. I'm quite curious what other medieval beliefs you hold."

"N-no, it isn't necessary, my apologies sir, I mean. Mr. —"

Anthony sneered. "Viscount Maddox at your service." He reached across the table and shook the man's hand.

The man paled and went equally limp in Anthony's clutches. Not feeling the least bit guilty that the sorry excuse for a man had fainted, he dropped him to the floor and left the notes scattered about the man's person.

"He'll be fine, just had a good scare is all." He winked at Bridget and noticed a shaking girl next to him.

"Devil take it, are you going to faint too?" He reached for the redheaded girl, but she shied away and shook her head all the while mumbling something about the dangers of the written word.

Bridget followed him out of the bookshop and promptly ordered her maid to see her friend, whom she called Gemma, to the carriage. Anthony was shocked to see the resemblance in the two girls' features. Not that Gemma was by any means more beautiful than Bridget, but the ladies could easily be sisters.

"Thank you." Bridget's voice broke his thoughts as his eyes came back to the street where they stood.

"Oh, no thanks are necessary. I should be thanking you for such… wonderful reading. I shall stay up all night." He joked as he held the books prisoner behind his back.

"May I have them please?"

"Will you promise not to yell or grab my shirt collar, or pull at my cravat if I don't give you exactly what you want all the time?"

Bridget shifted nervously from one foot to another. Her beautiful face was still flushed, and Anthony cursed himself and the rules he had to abide by. Nothing would please him more than to reach out and pull the infuriating woman into a kiss.

Any woman in possession of half as much passion as she had was a woman he wanted to keep. Dangerously close to breaking the rule, he took a step back and held out the books between them.

"I cannot promise," Bridget said taking the books and stepping closer to him. "You might someday give me cause to yell or grab your shirt collar or pull at your cravat." Her head leaned forward ever so slightly. Anthony's eyes were drawn to her bee stung lips as well as her rapid breathing. He knew that look.

Devil take it, he saw that look on a daily basis. She

wanted him to kiss her.

He waited for her to move closer.

She did. No doubt she was testing him. Well, there was no chance in Hades he was going to give into that type of temptation. If the little minx indeed thought she could so easily break the rules, then she could burn with desire for all he cared! If he as much as grazed her lips without warning she'd be more likely to take a dagger to his favorite part of his anatomy than forgive him. It wasn't playing fair. Perhaps it would be best for her to know what it felt like to want something so bad she could taste it, but have no means by which to satisfy that hunger.

Deciding to let her suffer, he heaved a sigh and then promptly knocked the books to the ground between them.

"Oh, apologies, I'm so very clumsy at times."

Bridget knelt down to grab both books, the pallor of her face deepened into a bright crimson that matched her hair.

He took her hand within his and bestowed a kiss upon it. "Good day."

Anthony tipped his hat and walked in the opposite direction, leaving a fairly seething Bridget behind.

Chapter Nine
The Best Defense

To say Bridget was angry did not begin to describe it. Abandoned. Humiliated. Rejected.

Furious.

And arrogant Lord Maddox — the impossible, infuriating beast of a man — was every whit the enigma. One moment he was swearing an oath to keep his hands to himself, the next moment he seemed to have eight of them, and every one acted as a homing pigeon bringing messages of desire straight to her core. As if that wasn't enough, when she actually wanted him to kiss her, he left her twisting in the wind.

A fresh surge of indignation burned through her again. She climbed the stairs to her rooms, slamming the door behind her with a fury.

This ridiculous bargain was more trouble than it was worth. True, Aunt Latissia and Uncle Ernest had stopped hovering about at the social functions, but the viscount had hardly kept up his end.

In fact, the only thing for which Bridget could rely on Anthony was that he was completely unreliable. But that was just like all the men she had ever known. Why did this one disturb her so much?

A knock sounded on the door, and a downstairs maid entered with a bouquet of fresh flowers.

"Begging your pardon, milady. These arrived for you a few minutes ago." She placed the bouquet in a crystal vase on a small table, turned to Bridget, and offered an envelope.

"Thank you, Lily," Bridget said as she accepted the note, tempering her bad humor in the presence of the servant, though she was certain signs of her rage were still evident on her face.

Lily nodded but made no move to depart.

"Is there something else, Lily?" Bridget asked.

"I'm to wait for a reply, milady."

"Very well." Bridget retrieved her letter opener from the drawer of the table and slipped the blade through the flap of the envelope, making a clean slice across the top. The note was from Viscount Maddox.

> *I would be delighted if you would join me tomorrow*
> *afternoon for a picnic in the park.*
>
> *A.B.*

It was enough to incite a fresh burst of fury through her. The man was so exasperatingly arrogant. No apology. No humility at all. He simply assumed she would be unable to refuse him. In his defense, she guessed he could have mistaken her body language as something other than what she was portraying. But he was a rake! Well, perhaps not a rake. He wasn't nearly as debauched as other men in the *ton*, but surely he knew the signs of a woman who wanted him! She bit her lip in thought.

Ah! The perfect revenge. Let him experience the rejection he so callously doled out. She would repudiate his every advance. Let him lose his bet. What was it to her?

With great aplomb, Bridget took a sheet of stationery from her desk and penned a reply to the viscount.

Regrettably, I am unable to accompany you on a picnic tomorrow.
I shall be taking my lesson on the pianoforte.
B.D.

She folded the note and slipped it into an envelope. Then a wonderfully evil thought occurred to her, and she spritzed the envelope with her favorite bottle of strawberry-scented perfume, sealed it, and handed it to the maid with a wide grin.

"Please have this delivered to the viscount right away."

Lily nodded and took her leave.

Bridget eased into her wingback chair and picked up her new copy of Miss Wollstonecraft's masterpiece. Suddenly, she felt ever so much better.

Chapter Ten
A Strategic Turn

Anthony hadn't attended one of Lord Byron's readings in an age. And although he wasn't supportive of how the ladies seemed to salivate in the man's infuriating presence, he did expect a few other poets and political minds to be attending the afternoon soiree. So he attended knowing it would be an advantageous time for him to discuss political matters before Parliament commenced again.

It also wouldn't bode well for him to sit at home and mope, especially since Bridget had refused him. The minx had even sprayed the letter with perfume. Well, he wasn't some simpering miss of a woman. He was a man. And it was his duty, his responsibility, to make sure this meeting was well attended and supported. He would, perhaps, stroll by Bridget's home at a later hour, mayhap under the cover of darkness so nobody could see him. He could even wear a black cloak and hat. Satisfied, he glanced around the room.

As predicted, several powerful political figures attended. Anthony and Sir Wilde made quick work about the room, enjoying the talk of politics more than that of the tedious events of the London Season.

"And do you agree? Should we truly be allowing those in trade into our higher circles?" Lord Jethrow asked, purely outraged that Anthony, along with his brother, had already been dipping into trade more than was acceptable for any noble.

"Yes, we cannot simply rely on our tenants forever," Anthony replied. "Nor is it wise to simply drink away one's life in hopes that the family coffers will replenish themselves." He took a sip of his tea amidst several grumbling gentleman near him and scanned the room.

His eyes fell on a beautiful redhead — his redhead. Bridget turned in his direction a look of pure excitement on her face. Not that he was surprised. Any sort of political soiree where she might brush shoulders with the freshest minds seemed to be her exact cup of tea. What surprised him… nay, irked him, however, was the girl wasn't at home pining away for him.

Her gaze appeared to take in the room as well, but she squinted in confusion when she noted his presence. Nothing like her obvious vote of confidence in his intelligence.

"Let us begin!" a voice announced from the front of the room. Anthony returned to his seat next to Wilde and smiled when he noticed Bridget taking a seat behind him.

"Thank you to all of our supporters and patrons, and many thanks to one of our biggest sponsors, Viscount Maddox!"

The room erupted into applause as he briefly stood and took a quick bow around the room, pleased that Bridget's mouth had dropped open and then snapped shut.

Trying not to gloat, he took his seat and smiled to himself. He hadn't planned for her to be there, didn't even know she would be attending. But it had worked in his favor. Served her right for making snap judgments about his character. She had presumed he was a rake, but there was so much more to him than what could be seen at first glance.

He was surprised he hadn't thought of this strategy before. Let her see him for whom he was outside of the balls and the parties. It certainly couldn't make matters worse.

The lecture and reading droned on. At its completion, a standing ovation was given to that dandy, Byron, and everyone was dismissed.

"How did you know?" Bridget's voice interrupted the clapping and scraping of chairs as people began milling about.

"Know what, precisely?" Anthony turned to face her.

She glared at him with her hands on her hips. "That I was going to be here! You would have had to have been planning this for months!"

"Sweeting, even I, infamous seducer that I am, do not plan such things so far in advance. I'm on several committees, including this one. I financially back several of the political figures you read about in the books you apparently steal or beat out of the bookseller, and to be honest, I'm a little put off that you would believe I would do all this for your sake alone."

He hadn't meant for it to come out as the scolding that it did and inwardly winced for the set down he knew he was to receive.

Instead Bridget opened her mouth to respond but shook her head, an embarrassed shade of red graced her cheeks. "Apologies, I truly had no idea. I didn't mean — well, of course I didn't mean to suggest you would go to such lengths to secure my favor, but—"

"Sweeting." Anthony leaned in so he could better smell the lavender. "You are right to assume I would go to the ends of the earth for you. Make no mistake about that. You just happen to be wrong as it pertains to this specific instance. Now..." He pulled back to put the space propriety demanded between them. "May I call upon you tomorrow for an afternoon stroll?"

"Um," Bridget hesitated. A more stubborn woman he had never come across! "I'm sorry, my lord. I have a previous engagement tomorrow afternoon."

"Yes, of course. Perhaps another afternoon." Anthony bit his lip in confusion.

"I will be attending the Hawking ball tomorrow evening. I'll save you a dance if you wish it."

"I do. Thank you. Until tomorrow evening then." He kissed her hand and walked away scratching his head. So this is what true rejection felt like? Not the cat and mouse type of rejection he was used to where women played games in order for him to chase them. But true rejection in which the woman lied in earnest to keep him away.

Somewhat depressed, he walked over to the nearest sideboard and poured himself a brandy.

Bridget's unmistakable laughter glittered on the air, causing him to nearly choke on his drink. Blast! Who could possibly be making her laugh?

Frantically, his eyes searched the room until they fell upon Bridget and Wilde sitting near the alcove huddled in secret conversation.

Wilde wore the most ridiculous and besotted grin on his face. And Bridget, well, Bridget seemed to be playing right into it! Her hand reached out and patted Wilde's thigh. His thigh!

Outraged, Anthony set the glass down and started toward the two, but Byron stopped him. In that moment, he wanted nothing more than to cut the man. Instead he bit off his rage and fell into civil conversation, all the while keeping an eye trained on the corner.

By the time the conversation with the infamous poet was finished, Anthony was fit for Bedlam. He made a beeline for the corner only to find Bridget was nowhere to be seen.

Wilde however, still stood in the corner, a lovesick grin painted wide across his face.

"Wilde? Where is Br — Lady Bridget?"

"Hmm?" Wilde's smile broadened. "Oh, Lady Bridget? She has taken her leave."

"Right." Anthony stared at his friend for a few more minutes, noting that Wilde looked everywhere but Anthony's gaze. "Say, are you unwell?"

"Not at all!" Wilde laughed nervously. "Everything is perfect." He patted Anthony absently on the shoulder and moved past him. Something was amiss with Wilde. He didn't know what, nor did he have time to figure it out.

Bridget seemed to be avoiding him. But why? He hadn't crossed any lines and to be perfectly honest, she should be rewarding him for not taking advantage of her earlier when she tried to kiss him.

Blast! Maybe that was why she was being so skittish! Could she possibly be angry with him?

Anthony swore under his breath as another man approached to engage him in conversation.

Chapter Eleven
Foiled

The following afternoon, Anthony decided a visit to White's would help to clear his head. He glanced at his curricle parked outside Ambrose's townhouse. The thought of sitting for the jolting ride made him cringe, perhaps it was because after a long night without any word from Bridget, he had sought company with a bottle of whiskey. His head still pounded.

"A walk would do me good," he said aloud and began his hike down the street, hobbling uncomfortably as he went.

It was a longer walk than he had anticipated, considering he had every intention of going to White's, but for some reason — one he wasn't ready to come to grips with yet — he made his way toward Bridget's house. True, she had said she couldn't meet him this afternoon, but that didn't mean he couldn't casually walk by, just in case she happened to be looking out a window.

Was he truly walking the three miles to her residence in order to stalk her? Apparently. Because his feet continued in that direction seemingly of their own accord. And the closer he came, the broader his smile grew. As he rounded the corner, a very happy-looking Wilde approached from the direction of Bridget's residence.

"Wilde?" Anthony called out. "What the devil are you doing here?"

Wilde paused a look of pure horror flashed across his face. "Isn't it obvious? I was out for a stroll."

"So far from the park?" Anthony squinted and crossed his arms.

"What are you doing out this direction?" Wilde countered.

"If you must know," Anthony looked away and lifted his arm into the air, "I was taking some fresh air." He made dramatic effort to breathe in the London fog and coughed aloud.

"Three miles from your residence?" Wilde lifted an eyebrow.

"I needed a lot of… air."

"Right, I'll just leave you to it then." Wilde stepped around him and shoved his hands deep into his pockets as he strolled away.

Anthony felt suspicious. Truly there was no reason for Wilde to be on this side of town. He knew nobody in residence, except…

No. It wasn't possible. Was it? Would Bridget be meeting Wilde? And for what purpose?

He rested against an iron fence for a moment in thought and turned the corner to stare at Bridget's house. To his chagrin, he didn't even try to hide his interest, just stared wide-eyed at the house that held the woman who had caused him to drink himself into a stupor the previous night.

Much to his surprise, on the side of the house directly before him, a gloriously exposed ankle peeked out of the second floor side window.

Transfixed, he watched as another ankle followed and

then what appeared to be bed sheets tied together. A fall from that height wouldn't kill a person, but serious injury would indeed result. His protective instincts kicked in, and he scurried as fast as his body would allow to the side of the building and called up.

"Are you sure you should be doing that?"

With a squeal the girl lost her footing as well as her grip on the sheets and began to tumble out the window, heading straight for him.

"Blasted — Umph!"

Again on his backside, and again in such pain he believed he heard angels calling him home, Anthony blinked twice to see what and who had fallen on him.

An unladylike string of expletives flew from the woman's mouth. She pushed away from him and shoved him down, unfortunately back onto his bum. The squeal of pain that erupted from his lips was anything but masculine and quite reminded him of an ostrich dying.

"You!" the woman shouted.

He looked up. "Holy Mother of—"

"You could have killed me!" Lady Bridget interrupted with an ear-splitting scream.

"I wasn't the one crawling out of the window!" he snapped back.

"No, you merely waited until I was halfway down and then startled me!"

Well, when she put it that way...

"Foul!" Anthony argued. "I was trying to keep you from climbing down! I didn't want you to fall."

"Well, congratulations, my lord, you accomplished your task admirably I'd say!"

"I..." Anthony snapped his mouth shut. What was she wearing?

"What in heaven's name are you wearing?"

Lady Bridget looked down and blushed. "That's none of

your concern."

She made a move to pass him but he grasped her wrist. "It is my concern when a young woman of genteel breeding leaves her house unaccompanied and wearing the attire of a footman."

"Odd, considering your preference for blindness, I'm surprised you see anything at all!" Her eyes blazed with fury. "Now, sir, let me pass."

"I don't believe my conscience will allow that, my lady." His grip tightened on her wrist.

"Do you mean to insinuate you have one then?"

Anthony smirked, trying to hide the pain radiating through his body. "Only when it seems prudent."

Her nostrils flared.

His breath grew ragged as his eyes boldly scrutinized the way her pantaloons hugged her thighs. No chance he was going to let her gad about the streets of London on her own. Any man with the benefit of functional eyes could see she was a woman!

"I ask you again, sir. Let me pass."

"And I'll tell you again, my lady — or shall I call you *boy*? Yes, *boy* seems accurate, since you're acting immature and senseless — I will not let you pass until you permit me to escort you to your destination."

The girl offered him an over-sweet smile, but he could plainly see she was mocking him. "Fine. But I warn you, you won't like what you see."

Anthony's eyes scanned her form again as she stepped around him. "Oh, I doubt I'll take any offense from what I see. Of course, what I *hear* — that might be an entirely different story."

"Hmmph." She thrust her nose in the air with disdain and stalked in the general direction of his townhouse, working perfectly to his advantage.

Awkwardly, Anthony fell into step beside her. Never

offering his arm, for what would people say if they saw him escorting a young boy? Even if the boy in question was actually a beautiful woman ripe for the taking.

They walked in awkward silence all the way to the end of the block. Bridget stopped at the house on the corner and followed the path to the front door, and without knocking she let herself in.

"Are you mad! You cannot simply let yourself into someone's house! Whatever would people think? What would they say—?"

"Bridget, my dear, is that you?" a man's voice called.

Anthony cursed. "A man? You're here to meet a man? And dressed as a boy? Could this possibly get worse? You shun my attentions for another?"

"Bridget?" The voice was hoarse and weak.

"Merciful heavens! I will never live this down," Anthony mumbled to himself as he followed the girl around the corner.

His eyes fell on an elderly gentleman who seemed to have one foot in the grave. "Ah, Bridget, my dear, are you ready for your fencing lesson?"

"I was wrong. It just became much worse." Anthony began to perspire as Bridget shed her coat and rolled up her sleeves. Smooth fair skin peeked out from her white shirt, causing his nostrils flare in agitation or arousal — he wasn't quite sure which, but he was certain the temperature in the house just spiked at least ten degrees. And where was the blasted butler with refreshments?

"And you are?" the elderly gentleman asked.

"Viscount Maddox at your service." He bowed curtly before the man and waited.

"I'm sorry, Lord Travis. He insisted on following me."

"How fortuitous, my dear. You shall have a sparring partner."

"Sparring partner?" Anthony repeated and began to laugh. "Surely you jest."

"I never jest." The man made no move to smile or breathe, it seemed.

"Right, then." Anthony shifted on his heels. "So I'll just..." He didn't finish the sentence. Instead he silently cursed his brother and Wilde as he shook off his jacket and readied himself for battle... against a woman. The very woman he was supposed to be winning.

Truly, the odds were not in his favor.

"En garde!" Bridget yelled.

Anthony cursed again and momentarily considered running for cover. But a look of pure satisfaction danced across Bridget's flawless face. So he pointed his rapier in her direction and swore to make her sorry she ever challenged him in the first place.

At the old man's signal, Bridget began an intense attack, driving Anthony back several steps. It was all he could do to parry the furious blows she swung at him. What had he gotten himself into?

She was good.

But he couldn't let her think he was impressed. Nor winded. Nor concerned he might just lose. Blast, if he wasn't all of those things.

His opponent settled into a graceful rhythm. Her ease of movement, as though the rapier were a mere extension of her arm, was as natural as a lithe reed in the wind. Their dance continued. Anthony drew back a step before her attack, making a desperate attempt to focus on the necessary defense. But she made it nigh impossible.

A steady cadence of the clash of steel served to lull Anthony into a hypnotic state, one to which he was willing to submit when combined with the entrancing vision of his Bridget straining against the well-fitting breeches and gentleman's silk shirt.

With a rakish lift of his brow, he thrust his rapier into the loose fitting fabric, absolutely delighted with the loud rip of her shirt. With a yell, she charged him, but he sidestepped her and thrust his rapier again, this time to the left, finishing his rather artful tear of the shirt, revealing quite a lovely white corset underneath.

"Hmm..." He winked. "I had you tagged for a more colorful girl. Red hair, certainly you would have red—"

"You rake!" Lady Bridget's rapier came down on his. The steel clashed as she backed him up against the wall. He turned and, with a thrust, pushed her away from him and lightly tapped his rapier on her bum.

Her eyes blazed with fury.

So he obliged himself again. A very unladylike roar erupted from the woman's throat as her rapier whistled dangerously close to his face.

Rebellious tendrils of her fiery red hair sprang out of her tight braid, framing her ivory face, now flushed with exertion from the bout. And the flame in her sapphire eyes held him captive, a grave distraction — in a true duel to the death, he would have already lost his life. In this case, the price was much dearer. But Anthony knew it was too late, for he had long since forfeited his heart.

"Point!" The old man's announcement rang out an instant before he felt the sting of her blade, drawing Anthony abruptly from his trance.

He caught the haughty smirk gracing her lips for the briefest of moments. So she wanted to play, did she? Her obvious joy at besting him, made him want to strip her of the rest of her remaining clothes. That would teach the minx a lesson.

Again they engaged. When the lady attacked, Anthony gave way. When he aggressed, Bridget retreated, their steps as well timed as the most complicated of dances. The parry of blows and the singing of their rapiers through the air — the palindrome to which their hearts beat in rhythm.

"Lady Bridget," he began as he fought off another of her

hostile onslaughts. His breath was labored and perspiration soaked through his shirt. He wasn't sure what was causing him more distress, the lust pounding through his blood or the fear of accidentally stabbing the woman he wanted as his for eternity.

"Point!" Lord Travis bellowed again, interrupting Anthony's train of thought.

He was losing pitifully. He never lost. The thought of such a desperate humiliation — to lose to a *girl* — it was repugnant to his every male sense. If Lord Travis said point one more time in reference to the lady he was going to throw his rapier at the man.

Anthony glanced at Lady Bridget, noting the smile on her lips. A shot of adrenaline surged through him and he began his attack, forcing his opponent back while keeping his gaze locked on hers and allowing a smack of hubris to play on his own lips.

Bridget drew back, parrying his assault with a single raised eyebrow as if amused but with not so much as a hint of concern. Her casual defense disconcerted him, but he pressed forward, rearing her into a wall with every ounce of his remaining strength.

Their rapiers deadlocked, and Anthony leaned forward, using the advantage of weight to hold her there, unable to retaliate or regain her position. She pushed and fought against him, but he wouldn't relent. He could feel the pounding of her heart against his arm, and the desperate grappling for air as her chest rose and fell with her ragged breath.

His gaze dropped to her parted lips and felt himself drawn toward them by an undeniable force. Still her eyes held no fear, but all the more a fire danced behind the deep blue crystals threatening to consume him if he came nearer.

Mere inches from her sculpted lips, his breath ragged with gasps for air, he whispered, "Do you yield?"

Her gaze bore into him as if tunneling through to his very

soul, and he knew he could keep himself from her no longer, no matter their agreement.

Somewhere in the haze beyond the universe that held only the two of them, he thought perhaps he heard someone shouting instructions in Latin. Alas, he saw only the lady before him trapped in his arms, so the necessary proficiency to translate the words was far beyond his conscious reach in that moment.

He would kiss her again. As he had dreamed of doing since laying eyes on her crawling out of that blasted window. And to the French with anyone who would stop him.

As he closed the distance between his lips and hers — so close to his goal — amidst her rapid heavy breaths, she whispered hotly against his mouth, "Never." One deft roll beneath his arm, and she was free of his grasp, masterfully slicing the air with furious steel as he struggled to regain his footing and his comprehension of the sudden turn.

It was then he had his epiphany. There in the throes of a desperate bout with an unbeatable foe.

He didn't want to win the contest.

There was only one thing he wanted.

One prize that mattered to him.

Her next offensive maneuver drove him back to the table where the old man sat, taking his afternoon tea. The unyielding structure behind his legs took him by surprise, stealing his balance and causing him to flail wildly in futile effort to recover. Down he crashed onto the table, launching a platter of fresh fruit into the air, which pelted him like brightly plumed hailstones upon their descent.

The next thing he knew, Bridget, flushed and breathless, stood over him, her blade at his throat. With the other hand, she reached to his chest to grasp one plump red strawberry and lifted it to her mouth. Sealing her lips about the circumference of the ripe sphere, she incited his desire for her. His heart made a valiant effort to burst from his chest — no doubt longing to leap into the arms of its true conqueror.

She broke off the seductive bite and held the remaining portion toward him with an expression of innocent inquiry. "Strawberry, my lord?"

Yes, she was trying to kill him, mocking him again. But this time he would not be put off so easily. With a slow deliberate hand he nudged her blade aside, seized the wrist of the hand offering the offending fruit, and pulled himself upright.

"I believe I will," he replied.

Before she could offer any resistance, he slid a hand around her waist and drew her in to his arms, planting his lips on her luxuriant mouth, still moist with the sweet juice. Somehow, though Anthony had hated strawberries all his life, in that moment he was certain— he would never satisfy his craving for them.

Lady Bridget's arms wrapped around his neck as he pulled her flush against his body. Her mouth was hot, so sweet he wanted to die. Pulling at her hips, trying to get her closer, he could feel the bones of her corset. He smiled against her lips and tugged at the remaining shirt, ripping it completely off.

She shrieked and tried to pull away, lifting her hand in threat of a solid slap. Anthony laughed and used his weight to push her against the wall. His rapier lay near his foot. He dipped his boot beneath the blade and tipped it up to his hand then held it beneath her throat. Her breathing was ragged, up and down her chest went against the steel of the blade. Boldly, his eyes caressed her body, and with one last show of passion, he leaned in and kissed her roughly on the mouth, sucking the sweetness of the strawberry directly from her flesh as his tongue traced her lips.

"I think I've found a new favorite fruit..." he whispered against her lips. "Do you yield?"

"Bravo! Bravo!" Lord Travis clapped in the distance.

"Haven't seen this much entertainment since the opera last year!"

With the spell broken, Anthony pushed reluctantly away from Lady Bridget. All too aware that in his lustful haze he had stripped the lady of some of her clothing as well as kissed her in front of a peer.

Lady Bridget flew from him to the desk. When she returned, she pulled a pistol and trained it directly at Anthony's heart.

"Ah, protecting your own virtue, how very noble," Anthony muttered all the while silently hoping the pistol wasn't loaded.

"Touch me against my will again, and I will find a reason to shoot you." She seethed.

Lord Travis chuckled. "My dear, if that was against your will, I'd be delighted to see the entertainments when you are fully participating. Now, be a good girl and put the gun down. It is time you return home."

Nostrils flaring, Lady Bridget pulled back on the gun and set it on the table on her way out the door.

Chapter Twelve
Foiled Again

The look on the viscount's face was enough to curdle her resolve. Their arrangement wasn't working the way it was supposed to be. And the more distance she could put between them the better. For the more that he pursued her, the more she wanted him to — the more she wanted to give in to everything she swore she would never give in to. Bridget wouldn't be her mother. She refused it with the very core of her being.

But now that she had experienced the taste of Anthony's lips, the feel of his tongue as it tasted the sweetness of her mouth — she knew she was done for, that to put distance between them would be futile.

For her heart was already engaged.

It beat for him.

And she wanted to hate him for it.

But all she could think about as she grabbed the jacket from the nearby chair and slipped it on, was that no amount of distance would be enough to shield her heart from the rogue.

"Bridget, are you sure you don't want a rematch?"

Anthony said behind her. How the devil did he sneak up on her so fast?

Anthony's arms came around her from behind as he fumbled with pulling the jacket closer around her body. "If you don't mind, I'd feel much better if we hired a hack for our return, wouldn't want anyone seeing you in your current state of—"

"Embarrassment?"

Anthony's arms froze around her. "I was going to say in your current state of perfection. What woman would be embarrassed about the fact that she can best a man with a sword, her wit, and her intelligence, I ask? Let me just call for one, I'll not be a minute."

With that he left her, and with him went all of her resolve. The rake had won, for her lips yearned for his kiss almost as much as her heart yearned for his approval.

Moments later, Bridget found herself tucked inside a hackney carriage dangerously close to Lord Maddox. And for once he appeared nervous. He who was normally brimming with an aggravating confidence sat fingering the seam of his breeches, seeming at a loss for words.

A heavy blanket of silence encompassed them as the moment stretched out. The hack jerked into motion, breaking the uneasy stillness.

A flutter of nerves wreaked havoc in Bridget's stomach when Anthony cleared his throat.

"This arrangement isn't working," he finally said.

"That rather seems to be your doing, my lord."

"Anthony."

"Anthony. Sorry," she answered. "You seem dreadfully incapable of keeping your end of the bargain." Of course, truth be told, she so wasn't anxious for him to observe the terms of their agreement anymore.

His gaze never left his hands as she spoke.

"I'm losing, you know."

Bridget scrutinized him for a moment. How could that be possible? She had acted her part at all times, pretending to be utterly besotted with him when under the eye of his brother.

Pretending. That was an amusing thought.

"Your bet? How is that possible? Other than your complete inability to keep your hands—" She stopped because his hands had suddenly captured hers. His sparkling green eyes seemed to swallow her whole.

"No, Bridget. Not the bet." His gaze drifted to her mouth. Bridget swallowed the tight knot stuck in her throat.

"Then what is it?"

Again he looked her in the eyes. The golden corona of his emerald eyes flashed with a brilliant flame. Bridget cursed silently. Somehow she already knew what he was going to say. And her heart resonated with the truth of it. Maybe he would kiss her, for once without being angrily provoked.

For their kiss during swordplay could hardly count for a kiss — an assault was more like it, and she couldn't blame him for allowing his pride to get in the way, after all, she was a woman, and she had nearly bested him.

That is, until he began shredding away her clothes.

Bridget waited for Anthony to do something — anything, for he was still holding her hands tightly within his. Golden green eyes stared at her lips until with a curse Anthony pushed away and ran his hands through his thick hair.

"I'm losing my mind, that's what I'm losing. I can't believe my inability to control myself. I mean really, I know it isn't a shock at all to you, but I'm quite appalled. I cannot even sit in a hack with you."

Anthony shook his head, obviously disgusted at himself, and Bridget wasn't sure if she wanted to laugh at him or slap him across the face. Couldn't he tell she was already invested? That she wanted him as desperately as he wanted her? She was *acting* angry! But Anthony was notorious for bringing such feelings to surface in Bridget. Either she was wearing down, or she had just lost her reasons for keeping him so far away from herself.

Heart pounding, she leaned forward, allowing her jacket to fall slightly open in the middle, exposing her corset and chemise.

"Are you insane?" Anthony yelled hoarsely and began cursing everything under the sun including jackets before closing his eyes and reaching forward grabbing at her jacket to pull it tight against her. Only, he didn't exactly grab the right thing.

"Devil take me.... Bridget... Blast, tell me I did not just—"

Anthony's eyes were still closed; his hands remained in a very inappropriate place. Bridget froze, waiting to see what he would do.

****

Anthony wasn't really sure what to do. To move his hands would be madness, to leave them there, well, would honestly have the same outcome.

What brazen notion did Bridget get into her head? And why the devil had she purposefully opened the jacket more? Especially considering he had just made such an eloquent speech regarding his inability to control his more carnal instincts.

Immobile and absolutely paralyzed, Anthony did the only thing he could think of doing, the only thing his blood demanded he do.

In one swift movement he reached behind her head and pulled her lips flush against his, once and for all breaking the promise he had previously made to her, knowing that this one selfish act could seal his fate without her forever, but not caring of the future, only the present.

And the way Bridget went so willingly into his arms.

What the...

A sigh escaped her pouted mouth as she opened up to him and wrapped her arms around his neck pulling his hard body against her softness.

Such sweet desire shot through him that he wanted to roar. Instead he settled for increasing the pressure of the dance and demanding entry into her mouth. Anthony's tongue swirled and pushed against hers, he couldn't help but think that any minute she was going to push against him and he would receive yet another well-deserved slap.

Oddly enough, the slap didn't come. To be honest, he was quite alarmed when the only jolt that forced him to stop ruining the girl was the hack coming to a stop at its final destination.

Slowly, Anthony pulled back and looked into Bridget's glazed eyes. Over what, a few weeks ago, would have been triumph in having succeeded in the bet, he felt nothing except loss. Loss of her warmth, the sweet taste of her tongue — it was all gone, and in its place, the stale London air.

"Don't go." The words tumbled out of his mouth before he could stop them.

Bridget smiled and pulled the jacket firmly back into place. "I thought this was your idea. Am I not to sneak back into the house without getting caught?"

Sneak, right. For some reason his body felt such loss at her leaving that he had forgotten the reason for their secret jaunt in the hack in the first place.

"Just, follow me then." He opened the door and helped her step out. If anyone saw them, or recognized Bridget, she would surely be ruined.

A slow smile crept across his lips as he tried to keep himself from breaking into a full-blown laugh. Oh please, God, let someone see them.

As if God had surely heard the cry of his heart, Lady Burnside's voice boomed from around the corner.

"Hurry!" Bridget grabbed his hand. "She'll see us!"

Moral dilemma. Should he ruin her and force her hand? Or be the romantic and take the high road, possibly facing a later rejection?

"Anthony!" Bridget tugged his arm tighter.

Decisions, decisions. Truly, would she be so upset? So horrified to be forced into marriage with him?

Lady Burnside yelled at her maid, her volume told them she was drawing closer.

"Anthony!" Bridget said his name like a curse.

"Oh fine." *Blasted conscience!* He pushed her in the opposite direction toward the back of the house, just in time for Lady Burnside to come around the corner. In one movement, he thrust Bridget against the fence. Lady Burnside's dog ran toward Anthony's heels. On instinct he crushed his lips onto Bridget's in hopes that her aunt would want nothing to do with such a vulgar display.

He hadn't, of course, counted on Lady Burnside's reaction to his vulgarity. Naturally, he hadn't given a single thought to Bridget's attire. From the particular angle she still looked very much a footman.

And unfortunately, from that same angle, Anthony looked very much aroused.

Lady Burnside screamed such a horrifying loud scream that Anthony prayed God would strike the woman with lightning, or perhaps just remove her voice box altogether.

"My lord!" Lady Burnside patted her chest with her gloved hand. "A footman? Really? Is this why your attentions towards me have been so, so…?"

"Indifferent," Bridget piped in with a remarkably low voice that sounded extraordinarily like a boy's.

"Exactly." Lady Burnside's eyes narrowed. "I knew it had naught to do with any deficiencies of my own."

Anthony cleared his throat. "You see my interests lie elsewhere?" He shook his head even as he said it and fought the urge to step on Bridget's foot. She was laughing so hard he could feel her tremble behind him.

"Yes, well… You may trust me to be discreet, as always." Lady Burnside curtsied, picked up her dog, and scurried off, shaking her head and muttering to herself the whole way.

"Brilliant." Anthony swore once she was out of earshot. "Now your aunt thinks I chase footmen in my spare time!"

"Thank you?" Bridget offered in a cheerful voice.

Anthony scowled and turned to face her.

Cheeks rosy and hair mussed, she looked like a forest nymph, and he found that his eyes could not focus on anything save her bee-stung lips and wild hair.

"You are most certainly welcome, my lady."

"Bridget," she reminded him.

"Bridget."

Bridget looked down for a second before glancing back in his direction, a steely confident glint in her eyes.

"You win, my lord."

"Pardon?"

Bridget laughed. "It's apparent you truly haven't heard those words as often as you claim. Let me say them again, for it might be the last time you hear them from my lips. You win."

"What, pray tell, do I win?" He leaned in closer, taking in her alluring scent.

"The bet. You win. For the girl has fallen."

"Fallen?"

Bridget leaned forward and lightly spoke against his lips. "In love. The girl has fallen in love… with you."

In reverence, all Anthony could do, all he could *say* was, "Thank God." And his lips captured hers in another life-altering kiss.

Chapter Thirteen
Settling the Score

The realization of what this might mean to her didn't sink in until later that evening as Bridget readied for the ball. And as it did, she found herself a trifle confused.

On one hand, it was a completely new experience... being in love. She felt as though she could hardly keep her feet on the ground all afternoon. Her head swam with the fevered delirium Anthony's touch provoked. His intoxicating kiss.

On the other hand, her life as she had known it would never be the same—*could* never be the same. Every married woman she knew was exactly alike. Content to gossip and play cards on occasion with their social circles. Spending endless evenings watching and judging others from their matronly sidelines at the *ton's* events. Hiding their indiscretions from their likewise philandering husbands. She didn't want that life. Not even a little of it.

And then there was the matter of her father. In her heart she had always believed all men were like him. That not one would remain faithful if presented with half a chance. The thought made her stomach churn, for her heart was already in too deep. It was the very reason she had struggled to resist Anthony. To protect her delicate sensibilities behind a hardened and cold stone wall. A wall she had been certain no man in the world would prove worthy enough to scale.

Now she was exposed and vulnerable… and at a loss as how to proceed.

Bridget feared betrayal. Not because she believed Anthony would wish to hurt her, but because she knew her fragile heart would never recover from his rejection.

It was too late. She knew that with surety as well. Her heart had chosen Anthony, with or without her mind's consent. So what was left to do but close her eyes, leap, and hope he'd catch her?

It was time.

Time to stop fighting for control in a situation where there was none to be had. If Bridget was ever to be truly happy, she would have to play the odds.

As Tessa swept up her unruly red locks in the way only the lady's maid could manage, a sharp knock sounded at the door, slicing through her silent preponderance. Before she could answer, Aunt Latissia opened it and bolted through, ringing her lace handkerchief and groaning in dramatic fashion. Back and forth she paced, casting sidelong glances at Bridget as she went.

Finally, Bridget could stand it no longer.

"Is there something amiss, Aunt?"

The answer was a mournful sigh. Aunt Latissia stopped as if to speak, then shook her head in despair and set back to pacing the room.

Bridget pushed Tessa's hands away from her hair and rose from her place at the vanity table. She took a step closer to her aunt, cutting off her path.

"Aunt? You seem distressed. Has something happened?" Knowing her aunt as she did, Bridget was not overly concerned. Only trivial and meaningless things had the power to upset the woman, and then only if they inconvenienced *her*.

"Oh dear, dear, dear," the woman chanted, still shaking her head and lamenting.

Bridget denied her sudden impulse to grab the woman by the shoulders and give her a firm shake.

"Oh, Bridget! I have dreadful news. Just dreadful!" Her eyes were darting here and there, seeming unable to come to rest on any one point.

"Aunt Latissia?" Bridget put her hand on the lady's arm, bringing her flittering gaze into sharp focus on Bridget's face.

"Oh, Bridget. Bridget. You should sit down, my dear."

Bridget lifted an eyebrow in suspicion but sat down as she was told. Tessa promptly went back to dressing her hair.

Her aunt sashayed closer and reached out to touch Bridget's cheek gingerly.

"Bridget, dear girl. I do have some dreadful news. Concerning your Lord Maddox, dear. I—" She dropped her hand and went back to wringing her lace handkerchief, allowing her gaze to wander again.

"Aunt Latissia, please. Just say it."

"I caught the man in a secret tryst with — oh dear…" The older woman reached for the fan sitting on the vanity, opened it with a flick of her wrist, and proceeded to fan herself frantically. Finally she blurted, "A secret tryst with a footman! Here! Behind our very home!" Aunt Latissia closed the fan with a slap and threw her arms up in the air with an unladylike moan. "Can you believe it? Lord Maddox! No wonder he was so… *unfriendly*."

A sudden burst of mirth overtook Bridget, and she choked back a forceful laugh, covering her mouth with her hand to hide her amusement.

Fortunately, Aunt Latissia mistook the snort and gurgle as shock at the tragic announcement.

"I'm so sorry, my dear," she said, patting Bridget's arm. "I know you had set your cap for him. But alas, it is not to be."

Bridget's laughter strained through her tightly closed lips, sounding more like a heartbreaking sob. Naturally, tears followed — no doubt offering the appearance on an honest lament.

"There, there, girl. Put him out of your mind. My goodness, child, you act as though you were besotted with the gentleman. Now I say, dry your tears. We'll find you a fitting match yet. Sir Wilde, perhaps? He's been mooning about your heels like a lovesick fool these past few weeks. Will you not consider the gentleman?"

Bridget had yet to find her tongue and dared not speak lest she betray her delight in the whole misunderstanding. She merely covered her face with her hands and shook her head wildly.

"Well, perhaps you'll think better of the matter this evening. Finish dressing, dear girl, and put Lord Maddox and his propensity for footmen out of your mind completely."

At that, Bridget burst forth with another round of stifled laughter and turned quickly away from her aunt, leaving only the trembling of her shoulders as evidence of her amusement.

"Tessa, do stop standing there staring and make yourself useful! Help Lady Bridget with her gown."

The lady's maid, who had been gaping in silent shock at the entire scene leapt into action immediately.

Aunt Latissia muttered to herself as she made her way out into the corridor. "I know I gave my word I would be discreet, but the *ton* must know the truth. Perhaps an afternoon call to Lady—" The heavy oak door slammed shut behind Aunt Latissia as she stormed out.

****

Aunt Latissia had played her hand well. By the time Bridget and her sponsors arrived at the ball, the gossip buzzing in everyone's ears was Anthony's interest in footmen.

Bridget scanned the room for the viscount, eventually locating him in her customary hiding place behind the potted plants. Her heart raced at the sight of him.

"There you are, my lord," she said as she joined him. "Hiding?"

"Not at all. I am simply enjoying the beauty of our host's lovely greenery. It's not often I have time for such activities."

"I see. They are lovely." She glanced about him on the right and left then asked with a smirk, "Where is your footman this evening? Home with the children?"

His vengeful glower brought a smile to her lips. And then a playful glint danced in Anthony's eyes.

"No. In fact, I believe he's nigh at hand. No doubt sharpening his rapier in case it is needed to defend my honor from anyone who would wish to steal away my virtue."

"Surely he has nothing to fear in me, my lord. I assure you, my intentions are as pure as the driven snow."

"Now that is a pity," Anthony answered, sidling closer.

Bridget's heart leapt and set off at a hot pace, causing her breath to catch in her chest.

"Would you care to dance, Lady Bridget?" he asked, his gaze boring into her very soul.

"I don't know if that's quite the thing, Lord Maddox. After all, you are rather the scandal this evening. And a girl cannot be too careful in situations such as this."

"I suppose that is true enough. However, somehow I believe your attention can only help us both."

"Both of us? Correct me if I'm wrong, my lord, but it is not my reputation being mucked about amongst the pigs this night."

Anthony looked past her with a mischievous grin. "Perhaps you are right, sweeting." He shrugged and added, "It is just as well."

She regarded him with humorous suspicion. "Oh? And why is that, oh great Adonis?" The nickname seemed to take him off guard for a moment and his gaze returned to meet hers then dropped the short distance to her mouth. Her lips warmed in anticipation at his mere look.

"You're not wearing breeches," he said with a roguish wink. "Ask anyone here. Unless you're in breeches, you are of no interest to me whatsoever."

"Is that so? In that case I'm certain Lady Burnside will be only too happy to give up her skirts for you."

"Of that there is no doubt. The very thought is enough to put me off completely." A shiver seemed to run through him. "Which brings us back to the beginning. Since I am no longer chasing footmen, I find myself in dire need of a fair maiden with whom to dance in order to expunge my soiled reputation."

"And you wish for me to rescue you?"

He took her hand and hooked it around his arm, gazing into her eyes as he did so. "I am desperate for it," he whispered and led her onto the dance floor.

****

Bridget bit her lip, hiding her contagious smile, and nodded her ascent. Anthony half-expected her to abandon him near the foliage. Instead she courageously marched forth toward the dance floor.

The whispered speculation increased. Anthony had no experience being on the opposite end of the gossip. Usually discreet, his only flaw had ever been his propensity to impersonate the incorrigible rake.

Tonight there would be no such gossip. Shifting uncomfortably, he pivoted to face Bridget. With a sigh, he raised an eyebrow and offered her a roguish wink. She in return managed an amused smile.

As the dancing commenced the whispering grew even worse, until Anthony was so irritated he wanted to start listing names of women he had successfully seduced, but the whole idea of seducing any woman put a foul taste in his mouth.

And then he began to feel abashed, which was even worse than asking for help in his mind, because guilt spoke of true feelings, a conscience.

The idea that he had sought out other woman when the one he had always needed was now dancing with him was repugnant.

So instead of taking a poll, he managed to finish the dance and pulled Bridget flush against him.

"Anthony," she whispered. "You are causing a scandal."

"I'm proposing," he announced with far more confidence than he felt. And though he tried to hide the palpable emotion, his voice rose two octaves, betraying him.

Bridget's brow quivered slightly. "Are you now? And what are you proposing? Another of your vulgar deals, my lord?"

"Marriage," he said boldly, loudly, without hesitation. And then Anthony Benson, Viscount Maddox, kissed her in the middle of the dance floor. Stopping all gossip, all slander, and apparently every breath in the entirety of the ton as the music stopped and people gaped.

"Bravo!" A man clapped, and Anthony turned to see Ambrose chuckling and clapping like a fool while Wilde stood beside him with his arms across his chest, scowling with an inordinate passion.

The abrupt outbreak brought Anthony spiraling back into reality, and he remembered where he was. With a sheepish nod at his brother, he escorted a flushed Bridget off the floor.

Lady Burnside stormed toward them, fire in her eyes as well as anger etched across her weathered face. "You!" She poked Anthony in the chest. "How dare you ruin her! And right here in front of everyone! Without announcing your intention to marry her! After what I saw! And that footman! Well, I—"

"You are mistaken, Aunt," Bridget interrupted smoothly. "There was no footman."

"Do not presume to tell me, girl!"

"I beg your pardon, Aunt Latissia. I suppose in one sense there was a footman, but it was not a man."

Lady Latisssia's eyes bulged. "I know what I saw!"

"Perhaps," Anthony offered, mainly because he couldn't help it, "it would be well to have your sight checked, my lady. After all, in such advanced age, one should be careful to stay healthy and," he cleared his throat, "astute."

Bridget planted a sharp elbow squarely in his ribs.

Lady Burnside grew crimson and stormed away.

"Congratulations, my dear." Bridget's uncle approached and offered his hand. "I will expect you first thing in the morning, Maddox."

Anthony smiled warmly as he shook the offered hand. "Of course, Lord Burnside. I look forward to it."

"Well then, I'm off to look after my wife's health. No doubt she's having a fit of the vapors."

"No doubt," Anthony mumbled under his breath. "Bridget?" He offered his arm and made quick work of guiding her outside near the gardens.

The memory of his first botched proposal to Cordelia haunted him. It had gone so horribly wrong. He hoped to make this one a vast improvement. Perhaps ride a white stallion through double doors and proclaim his undying love. Certainly Bridget deserved more than *Please consider me an alternative to perpetual virginity.* Botched proposals seemed to be his forte.

In retrospect, he counted himself fortunate that Cordelia hadn't slapped him across the face in that first occurrence. Although in Anthony's defense, his plan to push her into his brother's arms had worked brilliantly.

Yet, as he faced Bridget now and moonlight danced across her face, he was overcome with terror that he was about to make a blunder of himself once more. He cleared his throat.

"Bridget." He grasped her hands and took another deep breath.

A small insect chose that inopportune time to fly into his mouth, sending him into a coughing fit and nearly to his knees.

"Heavens! Anthony, are you all right?" Bridget pounded him squarely on the back several times before he was able to speak.

And when words finally did pour forth, they were hoarse and awkward.

"As I was saying…" He coughed again. "Br—"

His mind went completely blank. What was her name? Anthony blinked a few times and tried again. "Bri—"

Was it Brittany? Brisket? He was so nervous he couldn't remember his own name let alone hers!

"Do you need to sit down?" She gave him a breathtaking smile and patted his hand like a mother would a small boy.

"No!" Anthony braced her shoulders. "I'm going to do this! It will be proper and romantic, and you shall cry. Women always cry, don't they? In a good way? When a gentleman professes his love and quotes that dolt Byron? Perhaps I should take a knee. Yes, yes, that's it!" Anthony coughed again and knelt in front of Bridget.

Ha! He remembered her name!

"Dearest B—"

Curse him to perdition! He had just had her name! How was it possible to forget it already?

His shoulders slumped. "In my head, this went much better."

Perhaps he was capable of having two horrid proposals in the span of a year.

"Pardon?" Bridget tilted her head, an amused smile gracing her lips.

"Truly, just last year, when I proposed to Cordelia—"

Blast. Had he said that aloud? Bridget lifted a quizzical brow. Anthony cursed and tried to make it better. "But it was only a ruse, you see? It didn't truly mean anything. After all, it was only in order to force Ambrose's hand."

"Let me see if I understand. You proposed marriage to your brother's wife last year?"

When she put it that way, it sounded dreadful. "It was heroic! Even if I did run into her, and she did manage to fall and ruin her dress, among other things. And you cannot imagine the ruckus it caused when Ambrose happened upon us in such a state of..." Anthony cursed aloud. Wasn't he supposed to be proposing? Not regaling her with tales of his romantic failures?

"This is different. You are different," he mumbled. "I didn't know. How could I have known that the one girl to steal my heart and the breath straight from my lungs would be the very one I had no chance — no hope of gaining."

He stood and leaned in close to cup her face in his gloved hand, hoping she couldn't sense the perspiration drenching them in his angst. "I'm an idiot. It's a known fact, just ask Ambrose." He let out a loud ragged sigh. "But I'm an idiot in love with the most intelligent, beautiful, and infuriating woman I have ever come across."

Bridget swiped at a tear slipping down her cheek.

"Will you do the honor of becoming my wife? Idiot though I may be?"

"Bravo!" Ambrose interrupted the beautiful moment, clapping his hands. "Such believable gusto in your acting, brother. To think you would go to this extent to win a stupid bet is beyond me."

"Ambrose?" Anthony groaned. "What do you think you're doing?"

"Saving this poor girl from heartache!" Ambrose looked like he was ready to punch Anthony in the face. His eyebrows furrowed — always a bad sign — and his lips were in a firm line, proving he was very cross.

"And how were you planning to do that, brother?"

"I shall inform Lady Bridget of the bet!" Ambrose roared. "She doesn't deserve this treatment, Anthony, and you know it."

Poor sod. Anthony should have notified his brother where his true affections lay, but Ambrose was doing such a lovely job of making a complete fool of himself that Anthony couldn't bring himself to step in with the truth.

"The bet?" Bridget feigned ignorance, lifting a curious eyebrow.

How he loved her. She was brilliant.

"My dear lady…" Ambrose paced in front of her, swearing for several seconds before continuing. "My idiot brother and I agreed upon a wager. A challenge. The object of which was to convince you to fall in love with him. I am sorry, Lady Bridget. I never meant for it to go this far. I certainly will not condone a proposal under false pretenses. The very idea that he would pretend to love you in order to emerge victorious in this is abominable! And for my part, I beg for your forgiveness."

"A bet!" Bridget screeched.

Ambrose groaned and covered his face with his hands.

"I cannot believe this!" She turned to Anthony and winked. "And you!" She poked him in the chest with a sharp finger. "Are most assuredly an idiot."

Anthony grinned as she continued. "But I insist you marry me, which is my right after your behavior. After all…" She leaned in and bestowed a warm, lingering kiss on his mouth. "I have grown quite fond of you. And find myself quite irrevocably in love with you… against my better judgment."

"What the—" Ambrose cursed again.

"Ambrose…" Anthony growled between kisses. "Go away." And he drew Bridget closer in his arms, desperate for the warmth of her feminine curves.

"Right," Ambrose mumbled, and then he disappeared.

"You'll marry me?" Anthony asked again as he pulled back slightly.

"Yes." She kissed him again. "But I was thinking."

"Mmmm?" Anthony found utter delight in nuzzling her neck and tasting her creamy skin.

"Since we've already fenced..."

Had her skin always been this smooth? This perfect? His tongue craved the taste of her.

"Perhaps, you can now teach me to shoot?"

A sudden chill overtook him. Shoot? Did she just ask him to teach her how to shoot?

"Absolutely not." He continued kissing her.

Bridget pulled away and tilted her head. Anthony moved forward to recapture her mouth, but she stepped backward.

"Ah." He chuckled and rubbed his chin. "Let me guess... No more kissing unless I agree to your terms."

"Well..." Bridget slowly circled him. "I know how much you like to win. Just think. If you teach me, I'll be horrible at first, and you can best me at something. We both know fencing isn't your sport."

Anthony caught her and pulled her to him once more as they stepped into the shadows. He bit across her neck. "Oh my dear, believe me. There are a few things I can teach you. I do have a sport. You just haven't been made privy to the game... yet."

Chapter Fourteen
Foul Play

Bridget was still floating late the next morning as she scurried about the study preparing for Anthony's visit with her uncle. She couldn't wait to see him again. It was the only thing on her mind.

In fact, she was so preoccupied that when Francis announced the arrival of Sir Wilde, it took several moments before she remembered she had arranged for a meeting between him and Gemma that same morning.

"Lady Bridget, I want to thank you once again for setting this up. The lady is so skittish I find it quite impossible to get her alone no matter what I try."

"Yes, Gemma can easily become distressed. You will keep that in mind, I hope, when you see her this morning. Won't you, Sir Wilde?"

"Of course. I would never do anything to hurt Lady Gemma," he answered with an earnest nod.

Bridget led him to the salon. "You can wait in here. Gemma will arrive shortly."

Sir Wilde began pacing immediately.

"Will you sit, sir?"

"No… no. I think not." He continued without missing a stride.

Well, she had no time to babysit Sir Wilde. There were too many things left to do. And Anthony would be arriving any moment. Her heart leapt in her chest at the thought of seeing him again.

"If you will excuse me then, I have some things to which I must attend."

"Of course…of course," he answered without so much as a glance.

Francis stopped her in the foyer. "Lady Gemma, my lady."

"Thank you, Francis. Please show her to the salon. I'll be with her presently. And, Francis?"

"Yes, ma'am?"

"Please let me know the moment Viscount Maddox arrives."

"Yes, ma'am." The butler pivoted and went about his business. Bridget rushed up the stairs to finish preparing for her visit with Anthony. Perhaps they would finally go for that picnic he had been so eagerly promoting for the past week. Or they could spend the afternoon discussing plans for their wedding.

It didn't matter. Just being with him was all she desired.

Bridget giggled. If anyone had told her at the beginning of the Season she would be giddy as a debutante over any man within a few short weeks, she would have had them declared a heretic by the Church.

Safe inside her room, she closed the door and slumped against it with a deep, contented sigh.

****

Anthony bounded up the steps to the Burnside residence.

No amount of pain in his backside would slow him down on this day. Yes, it seemed everything was falling into place quite nicely.

He allowed himself a deep soothing breath of air and knocked on the door. The butler, who should be expecting him, nodded and led him through the entryway. As Anthony passed the salon where Bridget had painted his portrait, a smile spread across his face. Remembering the silly banter — and the excruciating self control expressed, for he wasn't able to kiss her even though he desperately wanted to — he motioned for the butler to wait and walked over to the closed doors.

Just one peek. After all, Bridget wasn't one to gloat over her talent, who knows when she would actually show him the painting. Yes, he would allow himself one peek and she wouldn't be the wiser.

Anthony lifted his hand to open the door, but the butler cleared his throat. "My lord, if you will just follow me."

"One moment." Anthony's hand moved to the doorknob, then he shook his head. What the blazes was he doing? Gentleman didn't just roam about people's homes, peeking into their rooms! Clearly he was in need of a drink, or quite possibly he was out of his mind. The sooner he married Bridget the better.

And then...

He heard it.

Unmistakable. Even from this distance.

Wilde? What the devil was he doing here? His hand reached again for the door.

"Sir," the butler interrupted, "please follow me."

Anthony knew he shouldn't be rummaging through the house, but the sound of Wilde's voice on the other side of the door drew him, and he continued to twist the knob. A strange pang of apprehension burned in his stomach. Wilde had no business at Bridget's home.

He pushed the door open.

And froze.

Anthony's blood ran cold. For standing in the middle of the room was a redhead — his redhead — and she was kissing his best friend.

Wilde cursed and turned blood red.

"I'll kill you." Anthony seethed as he watched Wilde shield the woman in question. His pain was so deep, so life altering that his lips could not even utter her name.

"Whatever for?" Wilde yelled. "Was I not kissing her appropriately? Considering you were doing the exact same thing last night, I doubt it is you who should be pointing fingers, my friend!"

"We are not friends. Friends do not..." Anthony's rage was hardly in check; he lifted a trembling hand to his forehead and stormed out of the room.

Anthony reached the door then yelled behind him, "Name your second, Wilde! Pistols at dawn!"

****

The sound of Anthony's voice filtered up the stairs, causing Bridget's heart to take up residence in her throat. She took one last glance in her looking glass, pinched her cheeks, and rushed to meet him.

Her feet were moving so fast she was certain she would lose her footing on the steps and dive headfirst down to the foyer, so she forced herself to slow down. After all, he wouldn't leave without seeing her. No use breaking her neck on the day of their engagement.

Just as she reached the landing, she caught sight of her beloved viscount standing in the front entry with his back to her. A sudden sense of foreboding caught her off guard, and then she heard it.

"The engagement is off!" His pronouncement echoed

through the house so terribly it felt as though the walls would crumble around her. And most certainly, her heart already was.

He didn't appear to have seen her standing there, as though his statement was made to no one in particular and everyone all at once. It made not a whit of sense. Had they not been ridiculously happy mere hours before? Bridget knew she had been.

Unless...

It was all a horrible joke. An evil scheme. A rakish plot to defraud the heart of an impossible woman, to make her love him, then to turn the tables and remind her of the lesson she had long understood.

Men leave. The arrogant ones leave sooner.

Wasn't it just her pure, dumb, Irish luck that this one ripped out her beating heart and took it with him?

Bridget stared at the closed door long after the viscount had disappeared. Her body seemed frozen in place. One hand on the banister, one foot on the stair below, and one foot on the landing.

From somewhere worlds away, she could hear the stifled cries of a woman and the soft murmurings of comfort coming from a man. But neither were for her.

With great effort she pivoted on her heels and trudged back up stairs to her chamber, willing her own tears to stay and her heart to hold together until she reached the safety of her own room.

Chapter Fifteen
Replay

"Is he dead?" Ambrose mumbled, standing over Anthony.

"It's possible he thought he saw a strawberry and had a fit of the vapors," Wilde concurred. "Or perhaps he now understands what a pickle he's gotten himself into."

If Anthony had any strength left he would have punched Wilde in the eye or perhaps pelted him with a strawberry, the deadly fruit. Or a harder weapon, like an apple. Yes, an apple would do nicely. Instead he groaned and moved to his knees, using the table to pull himself into the chair.

"You weren't kissing Bridget." On one hand, he hoped Wilde had been kissing her, because then his behavior would have been acceptable, expected even. It would have been understandable that he would call off the engagement — shouting it through the manor, sending her a letter of accusation — to challenge his best friend to a duel, and when he realized he lacked the backbone to go through with it, to drink himself into such a stupor that his entire body felt like it was sinking into the ground. Men would have nodded their

119

approval and women would have whispered sympathetically behind their fans that his poor heart had been broken. But he had been wrong. And now?

Bridget would never forgive him.

With a shake of his head, he finally ventured to look into Wilde's eyes.

"It was Gemma I was… *speaking* with in the salon. The lady who holds my heart. Lady Bridget had kindly consented to aid me in my suit to woo her." Wilde took a seat next to Anthony and glared, his fists were clenched at his sides. The muscles in his jaw twitched with fury. "Now thanks to your bungling, she won't speak to me. The poor thing is so embarrassed. Convinced word will get out, and she'll be ruined. She's locked herself in her room and refuses to see any living soul other than her brother and Lady Bridget."

Anthony moaned. He could not have possibly made a bigger mess of things.

"I'd wager he'd do anything to take yesterday back, even if it meant eating a carriage full of strawberries," Ambrose said.

Idiot.

"I believe I have had my fill of your wagers, Ambrose." Anthony slid his fingers through his hair in anguish. "What have I done? I must go to her. I have to find her — to tell her I was wrong. Explain things. She shall be cross, but perhaps she'll understand."

"Ha!" Ambrose slapped his knee. "You obviously have not seen a woman scorned before. Cross? She shall be more than cross! You'll be lucky to escape her without losing your favorite appendage."

"Surely cutting off his right arm would be too drastic, even for this offense," Wilde offered.

Ambrose rolled his eyes. "Not his arm, you dolt. I spoke of his *favorite* appendage, though I'll grant you, not the most useful. No doubt Anthony would argue otherwise…"

Anthony groaned again and allowed his head to fall to the wooden table with a thud.

"Up you go." Ambrose lifted his brother to his feet and helped him stumble to the door. "Now, you must be careful not to make a bigger muddle of things."

"Just apologize and kiss her," Wilde offered.

"Yes," Ambrose agreed, pushing open the door. "And if she draws a pistol, just let her shoot. You shall both feel better."

"Let her shoot? And if she kills me?" He could hardly believe his ears. Ambrose thought this was a laughing matter!

"A woman with aim? Unheard of. I can't imagine she shall do any permanent damage, and if she does, you don't want to live without her anyway, do you?"

"Your concern for me is touching." Anthony's body throbbed with the pain brought on by a long night of consumption. "So, that's your advice?" he asked as he dragged himself into the carriage without aid. "Kiss her, apologize, and permit her to shoot me?"

Wilde and Ambrose shrugged in unison and climbed in behind him. "Do you have a better strategy?" his brother asked politely.

Of course not. Anthony was not the most eloquent when it came to saying pretty words during times of great importance, though he was smooth enough when the moment was trivial.

Up until now, it had always been trivial. Nothing more than challenge after juvenile challenge. A simple case of puerile amusement for a University rogue.

But when it mattered, as it did now, he was no better than a bungling Frenchman.

"Where is she?" He grunted as his head fell back against the wall of the carriage.

"Hyde Park," Wilde answered. "She convinced Gemma to take the morning air with her."

"To Hyde Park!" Anthony hit the side of the carriage, and it rumbled down the road.

"Are you sure you should see her in your current state of…" Ambrose motioned to his brother's disarray.

"Stench," Wilde offered.

"I carry no fetid odors." Anthony murmured and stared out the window. At least he hoped he didn't. Perhaps the London air would counteract his eau d' drunkenness. He couldn't wait another minute to see Bridget. He had to convince her to take him back.

Ambrose was not so far off the mark. Truly, Anthony would prefer death to the knowledge that he had lost her forever.

The carriage came to a stop. Anthony jumped out.

Unfortunately, his boots tangled with one another, and he fell backward, flat on his bum. He cursed and rolled to his side.

"I changed my mind." Ambrose peered out through the door. "Just let her shoot you."

"Helpful." Anthony cursed and managed to clamber to his wobbly feet. Seeing double wasn't at all helpful as he hunted through the park for Bridget. He was glad for her definitive red hair; she would be much easier to spot that way.

Within a few minutes he located her strolling by the river with her likewise scarlet-tressed friend. Anthony lost no time strategizing his approach and marched straight toward Bridget.

"Bridget!" he called after her, gaining her immediate attention.

Her eyes narrowed when she spotted him, and with a word to her companion, she spun on her heel and walked in the opposite direction.

Anthony increased his pace until he was panting, likely sweating whiskey. "Bridget, wait! I must speak with you!'

"Your letter said more than enough, my lord. There is

nothing left to discuss." Bridget set her chin with firm resolve. Though her eyes appeared ripe with impending tears, he knew she would never deign to let him see her cry. Not after the things he had penned in his letter.

"It is not what it seems!" Anthony swayed on his feet and shook his head. "I thought it was you with Wilde, not Lady Gemma!"

At his announcement, Lady Gemma fell into a fit of hysterics and began to sob. With a shriek she scurried away with her face buried in her hands.

Perhaps he should have kept that morsel to himself.

"Bravo, my lord," Bridget said with a spiteful sneer. "You are able to make women weep with a mere word. Truly your skill of speech is legendary."

"Listen to me, woman!" Anthony blinked several times. "I love you! I thought Wilde had stolen you away! Surely you can't fault me. The appearance of — Admit it! You have been spending an inordinate amount of time with the gentleman!"

"I have nothing to hide." The malice in her blue eyes seemed to slice right through him.

This apology was not going as well as he'd hoped. Perhaps if he *had* taken the time to strategize... But he was desperate for her to see he was a victim of circumstance, and in that desperation, he floundered.

"You touched his thigh! At the reading. Your hand was — so I thought — that is, when I happened upon the two of you... of them... in the salon, I thought you were—"

"Offering my favors to your friend?" Bridget stepped closer to him, her face brilliant with the fury seething just below the surface, yet still she kept her tone even and cold. "It is a relief to know you trust me so fully, my lord. Your confidence in my character is most reassuring. Or is it that you were simply searching for any reason, any *excuse*, to allow you to leave?"

She was mere inches from him now, and he could feel her

wrath rising to a crescendo with each breath she took. "You believe me capable of betrayal. While you, on the other hand, did exactly what I expected you should do. I had hoped—" Her words seemed to lodge in her throat behind a lump of emotion.

Anthony knew, even in his inebriated state, he had achieved new heights of idiocy in this encounter, and he prayed the damage was not irreparable.

Still Bridget continued her cutting censure. "My heart didn't believe you were cut of the same cloth as other men, but I was wrong. The first time you were faced with an obstacle, you abandoned me. Just like my father."

Left speechless, Anthony watched as Bridget managed a brief emphatic nod before briskly retreating once again.

"Forgive me," Anthony muttered under his breath and returned ever so slowly to the waiting coach, where his twin brother sat with his arms crossed over his chest.

"You didn't take any of my advice, did you?" Ambrose shook his head in abject disappointment.

****

"I am not going to tell you I warned you, dear." Aunt Latissia lapsed into the lecture Bridget had known was coming. "But I did say he would not make a proper match for you. Did I not?" She shuttled her needle through the embroidery in her hoop as she shook her head with disdain.

"Yes, Aunt." Bridget had long since spent any emotional energy she might have used to argue with the woman.

The older woman stopped mid-stitch to scrutinize her. No doubt she was in shock at how easily Bridget had conceded. Her expression softened somewhat, and she patted Bridget's hand with what could almost be construed as a motherly tenderness. "There, there, dear. Not to worry. All is not lost, sweet niece. I daresay your Uncle Ernest can find you a suitable husband. He knows many worthy bachelors."

Bridget shuddered to think what her uncle might bring home to meet her. His social circle consisted mainly of men so ancient they appeared as though they could boast having seen Mr. Shakespeare's original productions at The Globe.

It made no difference now. She would marry whomever her uncle chose, to please her grandmother. Bridget offered a polite nod accompanied by a weak smile. "Of course."

"Ring for the maid, dear. Tea is the thing, I think, to chase your sorrows away."

Bridget set her needlepoint aside and jingled the bell on the side table. The maid scurried in and Aunt Latissia nodded to her.

"Tea and cakes, Geneva. The Lady Bridget is having a crisis." Then she addressed Bridget. "Would you care for some fresh fruit as well, dear? Perhaps some sweet berries? Yes, yes, I believe that's just the thing! Geneva? Off with you now, and step lively."

When the tea was served, Bridget studied the bowl of fresh strawberries and sighed. Her stomach churned. The last thing she wanted to do was eat... especially something that reminded her of the viscount. Her heart felt as though it had been torn out with some dull instrument. It was a pain she had hoped never to experience again.

She sipped her tea, hoping it would settle her stomach. Her eyes wandered to the corner where the finished portrait of Lord Maddox rested on the easel. It wasn't a perfect likeness, but she had captured his eyes nicely. The hint of mischief and mirth in their depths. The smack of hubris hanging on the corner of his crooked smile.

And then there was the strawberry he held in his hand, elevated as though presenting her with a gift. A perfect, ripe ruby just for her. And she wanted to reach out and pluck it from the painting to taste of its sweetness.

Something struck her then, something she hadn't noticed

LEAH SANDERS & RACHEL VAN DYKEN

even as she had spread the paint on the canvas on that ill-fated afternoon, which seemed an age ago. Tilting her head to the side, she scrutinized the berry from another angle.

Her breath caught in her chest and she squinted to be certain.

Yes. She was truly going mad.

The strawberry was shaped as a perfect heart. Only a fluke, surely. And yet, perhaps her traitorous hands had seen where her eyes had failed. Her heart in his hands or his heart offered to her. It didn't matter which. She could not escape the truth. She loved him.

The sound of Francis clearing his throat in the doorway startled Bridget from her private musings.

"My lady, Lord Maddox wishes to be announced."

Bridget's heart leapt to her throat again. The sound of her teacup clattered a silver rhythm against the saucer, betraying the tremble of her hands. She promptly set the teacup on the table and folded her hands tightly in her lap.

Aunt Latissia was caught off guard for what seemed like a mere instant. "That beast has some nerve showing his face here in our home after the scandal he has perpetrated, my dear. I have half a mind to allow him in, if only to see how far his boldness will go."

If Bridget hadn't still been holding her breath, she might have had the sense to protest. But her mind was hazy, and she was still busy trying to sort out what Francis had said.

With a predatory glint in her eye, Aunt Latissia ordered the butler, "Show him in, Francis. One does not leave a viscount waiting in the foyer."

At that, Bridget finally remembered to breathe.

When Anthony strode in, he looked a far sight worse than he had that morning. Though his gait was steady and sober, his eyes were etched with dark circles and several more hours of growth shadowed his face. Bridget indulged herself in sympathy for a brief moment, wishing she could forgive him, yearning to trust him again. But she knew the longing was in vain, for her heart was not safe in his hands.

"Lord Maddox! To what do we owe the great honor of your presence this afternoon?" Aunt Latissia crooned. The sound of her voice clung like thick lard in Bridget's throat, and she gagged back her urge to repudiate the teacake she had nibbled on only a few moments ago.

A sad smile glistened behind Anthony's eyes as he regarded her.

"I wish to speak with Lady Bridget," he said. His voice grated against his own throat as if too raw for use.

"I am not entirely convinced the lady wishes to hold counsel with you, my lord. She seems a trifle distressed at your presence."

"Perhaps the lady will answer for herself," he said, never releasing her from his glassy emerald gaze.

Bridget stared back at him in silence. Inside her warred two spirits. One demanded she guard her heart. The other begged her to risk it, promising rewards beyond her imagination. The first reminded her of her father's abandonment, insisting that all men behaved thusly. The latter whispered she deserved release from the suffering inflicted by one man's selfish ambitions.

In the end, confusion reigned, and Bridget felt ill equipped to handle it on her own. Her voice, however, seemed to speak independently of her will. Steady and firm without wavering, she answered, "I would speak with him privately, Aunt."

"Privately? Bridget, I do not think—"

"Francis may stay. Will that satisfy you?" Bridget suggested. Every word out of her mouth came as a complete surprise.

Aunt Latissia's mouth clamped shut, but she managed a curt nod before leaving the room, closing the door behind her with a huff. Francis moved to the tea table and poured two fresh cups.

"Thank you," Anthony said, taking the seat across from Bridget. He waved away the offered tea as his eyes implored her in earnest.

"Was there something you wished to say, my lord?"

He seemed to cringe at her use of formal address, but he did not correct her.

"I know I did not adequately express myself this morning. It seems no matter what I say it comes out all wrong. So I am somewhat fearful of what might find its way out of my mouth in this conversation. But I promised myself I would stick to the advice my brother gave me, because I ignored it this morning, and all Hades broke loose."

"A wise decision, I'm sure," Bridget snapped. Still teetering on the edge of indecision. The sense of a lack of control in this increased her irritation. "Will you come to the point, my lord?"

"Yes, of course." He glanced briefly at Francis before kneeling awkwardly in front of Bridget. A chill trickled down her spine, and she scooted further back in her seat to gain more space between them.

"It is entirely my fault. I'm sorry." He slipped his hand under her fingers and lifted it to his chest.

Bridget wrestled between the urge to kick him in his unmentionables or the desire to fall sobbing into his arms.

But she didn't have time to decide.

Before she knew what was happening, Anthony stood, pulling her to her feet along with him, whisked her into his arms, and planted a firm kiss right on her open mouth. Memories of their stolen kisses came flooding back of their own accord. His lips were smooth and tasted of cinnamon.

Shock hindered her from reacting. But Anthony seemed to know exactly what he was doing and took full advantage of her state of mind, deepening the kiss.

Her good sense came rushing back, filling her with fierce

indignation. She pressed both palms firmly against his chest and shoved with all her might, thrusting him away from her.

The rakish grin he wore drove her mind into a fury, and she reared back to deliver a swing that would possess the very real possibility of knocking the rogue quite firmly into the middle of next Sunday.

With all her might she aimed her closed fist at his perfect aristocratic cheekbone, but when he grabbed her wrist, absorbing all her power and rendering the assault useless, Bridget very nearly lost her mind with rage. With a roar, she wrenched her hand free of his grasp and stepped back, scouring the room for a weapon that would prove fatal to the arrogant sod.

She lunged madly for the teapot, thinking to send it crashing straight through his thick skull, but Francis was too quick and rescued the teapot from her reach.

The silver!

Her gaze raked the table for a sharp utensil. Only spoons! Blast! Where were all the knives?

Francis must have seen her eyeing the teaspoons, because he deftly removed them from her vicinity without so much as twitch in his perfectly deadpan butler expression.

"Give me something, Francis!" she bellowed in exasperation.

Without a moment's hesitation, the taciturn butler gracefully lifted the fruit bowl in one hand as if he were serving the royal table.

"Strawberry, milady?"

She could feel the wide evil grin spreading across her lips as she leveled her gaze on Anthony, who seemed to shrink into himself in terror like a frightened turtle.

"Why thank you, Francis. I don't mind if I do," Bridget replied, as she wrapped her fingers around an enormous handful of brilliant red ammunition.

Chapter Sixteen
To the Victor Goes the Spoils

Anthony entered Ambrose's townhome much like a dog with its tail between its legs.

Ambrose took one look at his brother and swore. "Well, that went well."

"Obviously," Anthony muttered as a squashed strawberry fell out of his jacket and tumbled onto the floor.

"I thought he didn't like strawberries," Wilde said to Ambrose. "It seems if he was so offended by said fruit he wouldn't take to bathing in it, which is the only conclusion I can draw given his state of dress."

"It is by my calculations," Anthony sat on a nearby chair and cringed when the sticky juice of the strawberry ran down his legs, "that when the lady could find no daggers, swords, or pistols, she became desperate and decided to torture me with my favorite fruit."

"She was successful, no doubt." Ambrose smiled and let out a chuckle.

"I shouldn't have kissed her."

"Idiot," Ambrose replied.

"Dolt," Wilde agreed.

"What did you expect me to do? I apologized! I went down on one knee, and I had this speech, truly it was a speech that would bring even Byron to tears, and then when I saw her lips and her face I lost—"

"—complete control of your mind, no doubt." Wilde shook his head. "If you do not fix this Gemma will never speak to me again! Women have to stick together, after all."

At Anthony's irritated look, Wilde apologized. "Well, it's not that I'm not concerned for you and the lovely lady, and yes perhaps I'm being a mite selfish, but saints alive, Anthony! I've never met a man so horrid at proposals and apologies in my life! And just this last year Ambrose apologized to Lady Cordelia by giving her a dead plant!"

"Now see here!" Ambrose roared. "I didn't know it was dead until after I gave it to her."

"That makes it so much better." Anthony closed his eyes while his brother and Wilde continued to bicker. They were both right. Perhaps he *should* allow the lady to shoot him — anything would feel better than the pain he was experiencing at present.

Bridget. She deserved the prince, the white horse, and the pretty words. She deserved it all, and he had kissed her instead.

Well, no more. He was going to do this right, even if it killed him, which to be truthful was a very real possibility.

"Right then." He pulled himself to his feet and strode purposefully toward the door.

"Where are you going?" Ambrose asked.

"To storm the castle," Anthony muttered and walked out into the afternoon air.

****

"Ahem." Francis cleared his throat once more, causing

Bridget to startle and jab her finger with the embroidery needle.

Her sharp intake of breath brought an almost apologetic glance from the somber servant. Involuntarily, she pressed the injured finger to her lips for a moment.

"Pardon me, miss. The Countess of Hawthorne to see you. Shall I show her to the salon?"

"Yes, thank you, Francis. I'll be with her presently." She laid her needlepoint on the table, stood, and smoothed the skirt of her afternoon dress. There was nothing she could do about her puffy, tear-stained eyes now, so she pinched her cheeks lightly and took a deep breath.

She made her way to the salon and pushed the doors open as she pasted her best fake smile on her face.

"Countess Hawthorne, what a rare pleasure!" The sentiment was forced and felt unnatural in Bridget's current emotional state, but she had no intention of making her personal trials the burden of a relative stranger.

"Lady Bridget." The sad smile behind the countess's deep blue eyes betrayed her intimate knowledge of Bridget's misfortune.

"Oh." Bridget stopped short of her perfunctory pleasantries. "I think I know why you're here." It seemed futile to continue with the expected social graces when she had no desire to perpetuate the acquaintance.

"I don't think you do."

"Please, Lady Hawthorne... I have no desire to re-live my humiliation for a third time today. Twice was quite suf—"

"Humiliation?" the countess interjected. "If that is the crux of it... I had thought it was somewhat deeper than mere humiliation. Lord Maddox didn't ask me to come, if that is what concerns you. I'm here of my own volition. My own culpability."

"I fail to see how Anth—Viscount Maddox's shortcomings are your fault, my lady."

"I didn't appear at your doorstep to talk about his shortcomings, though we both know he has many, like any other man in love without a clue of how to proceed when jealous rage takes over."

Bridget exhaled and took a seat. Lady Hawthorne joined her and laid a hand over Bridget's. "He loves you."

"I know."

"Do you?" The countess tilted her head. "I believe the problem is not that you doubt his love. You are allowing fear to cloud your judgment. I know something of fear. Love is frightening. It means entrusting your fragile heart to the one person with whom you are the most vulnerable." She nodded toward the portrait still on the easel behind Bridget. "That portrait. It is the very essence of what love is. Your very soul in the viscount's hands."

Her gaze returned to meet Bridget's. "Anthony spoke before logic became clear, and now he is trying to right a wrong. And who knows better than you and I what disastrous sentiments spill from that man's lips when he isn't thinking clearly?" Her eyes hinted at a smile. "A more stubborn man I have never met. He will not stop until he has your heart, and I promise you, Lady Bridget, there is no man more worthy."

"I wish I could share your certainty."

"You don't have to be certain—just willing to take the risk."

Chapter Seventeen
Beguiled

Anthony had always prided himself on being calculated and smooth with the gentler sex. Bridget brought out the exact opposite of what he had been all his life, and he found himself at sixes and sevens. But it was of no consequence now. He was going to prove his love to her, but if she was to reject him for the third time—well, it was possible — he would retire to the country. Perhaps buy a few hounds and hunt foxes until he became a bitter old man who yelled at small children.

The music was loud and didn't help his nerves one bit, but again, in his desperation, he didn't care. The moment he was announced, he quickly moved down the stairs. The Beckinghorn Ball was always well attended, but he wasn't there to socialize with every person in the crowd. The large ballroom with its flickering candlelight and lively dancing was stifling, but he pressed through the crush until he caught a glimpse of red hair.

This time he waited until she turned around, to be certain it was Bridget — his Bridget.

She smiled, but it didn't reach her sad blue eyes as she

spoke with Lady Hawthorne. The two seemed deep in conversation. They were also on the opposite end of the dance floor, which posed a problem.

Unless…

White horses, white horses, Anthony chanted to himself as he blazed a path straight through the heart of the dance floor, interrupting the flow of the dancers, who stopped to determine what he was at, whispering in his wake. The tumult on the floor distracted the musicians, who ceased playing to stare after him as he strode with purpose toward his goal.

"Lady Bridget." He cleared his throat and waited for her to face him. Her eyes welled with unshed tears. His arms ached with the desire to pull her to him, to comfort her, to take away the pain he himself had inflicted.

"I love you." The words were bold, loud, and rang through the silent room. He didn't care. She would know his heart if it killed him.

Bridget opened her mouth to speak, but he held up his hand to stop her. "No. Let me speak." He dropped to his knees in front of her, in plain sight of God and everyone. "I do not deserve you. I count myself lucky each time you grant me one of your smiles, as if you are giving me a priceless gift. Yet I feel guilty for taking something so beautiful. I feel selfish when I'm with you. I want you all to myself. The thought of any other man being on the receiving end of your smile drives me mad. I would kill any one of them given half the chance.

"I know I misjudged you… I could not have been more wrong. But you have also misjudged me. I am not like most men. Even though popular opinion would claim I too freely flirt my way through the *ton*. The truth is, no woman has ever possessed my heart… until now. And whether you reject me or not — and I pray you don't — my heart is yours to keep, for I would rather die than have any other woman hold it."

A tear slipped down Bridget's cheek.

"I cannot promise I won't be a fool. I cannot promise that

I won't be a devil to live with. But I will promise to honor and cherish you, to love you even when you pelt me with strawberries. To care for you and protect you, though we both know you're the better fencer… and I swear, to my utter ruin, I will teach you how to shoot. Even if it is the death of me. Forgive my blind stupidity, my love… and marry me."

"For heaven's sake, say you'll marry him before he says something horrifying," Lady Hawthorne whispered to Bridget with a teasing twinkle in her eyes.

All the room was silent. Bridget stared at Anthony, concealing her thoughts behind her blank expression as his heart pounded out of his chest.

"You will teach me to shoot?" Bridget finally asked, her voice hoarse.

"I promise."

"I…" Bridget's tears flowed freely now. "I love you."

Anthony wanted to kiss her… here in front of everyone, but he would not, for the act would ruin her before the whole of the *ton*. Instead, he merely smiled and brought her hand to his lips, but Bridget, her bright blue eyes suddenly alive with passion, launched herself into his arms, crushing her body against his, scandalously kissing him directly on the mouth.

"Now you shall have to marry me," she whispered against his lips.

"Whatever shall I do?" Anthony's voice was husky, giving away his desire to ravish the woman he loved so dearly.

Epilogue

"Where did Wilde make off to? It's almost time for the dancing to begin!" Anthony glanced around the room.

"He was just here," Ambrose chimed in. Cordelia and Bridget joined in the search; all four gazes roamed the room looking for their lost friend.

"Ah, er, ahem." Anthony coughed. "I believe I've found him."

"What the devil!" Ambrose exclaimed.

Bridget squinted. "I don't see him. Oh, goodness."

"Heavens, does he realize he looks quite..." Cordelia waved her hand in the air as if searching for the correct word.

"Mad? Scary? A trifle like a hunter stalking his prey?" Anthony finished.

For some odd reason, Wilde was hiding behind a large potted plant, his eyes fixated on Lady Gemma with such fervor the world could crumble around him and still he wouldn't blink.

Anthony tilted his head to the side for a better angle and laughed when he noticed all three of his companions stood frozen in the exact same pose.

"Does it help?" Bridget whispered with her head tilted.

"No," Anthony muttered. "No matter the angle, still looks like an idiot to me."

"Agreed," the others said in unison.

A booming voice interrupted their spying. "Where is he? I'll tear him limb from limb!"

Anthony turned to see the Marquess of Van Burge cutting a trail through the sea of people.

"Sir Wilde! Where is the blighter?" Lord Van Burge paused directly in front of Anthony. Without hesitation, all four of them extended an arm to point in the direction of the potted plants.

"My thanks." He nodded and went in pursuit.

"He'll probably kill him," Ambrose reflected. "And to think I thought the winter would be boring."

"Say, I feel a bet coming on." Anthony smiled. Ambrose met his gaze and matched his with a devious grin of his own.

Cordelia cleared her throat. "How about a wager of sorts?"

Bridget laughed. "I give him four weeks."

"—To obtain the object of his affection," Ambrose added, wrapping his arm around Cordelia.

"—And win her love," Anthony agreed, offering his arm to Bridget.

"After all..." Bridget hooked her arm in his and winked. "Anything can happen in four weeks."

About the Authors

Leah Sanders is the middle child in a family of seven children. As a true middle child she went from high school in Alaska to college in Florida, where she earned a Bachelor's degree in secondary education from Southeastern University. She also holds a Master's degree in educational technology from Boise State University.

She makes her home in Idaho with her husband and three children. By day she teaches English in a middle school. But after the kids are in bed, she will most likely be typing away on her laptop while sitting in her favorite spot on the couch.

Rachel Van Dyken loves to read almost as much as she loves to write. She resides in the Pacific Northwest with her husband and her dog Sir Winston Churchill. Although she loves to write contemporary romance, her heart will always be with historical and regency romances. Glittering balls and dangerous rakes hold her captivated like chocolate and Starbucks. You can follow Rachel on her blog, Twitter, or Facebook.

26030529R00090

Made in the USA
Charleston, SC
23 January 2014